"Drop your gu

The order came from the Mexican gunman as he jabbed his deadly weapon farther into Bobby Pearce's side. "Do it now, or I'll shoot the boy."

David McCarter believed the killer was desperate enough to follow through on his promise. He opened his fingers and allowed the Browning Hi-Power to drop to the landing of the fire escape.

"Now what?" McCarter asked as he leaned back against the rusted iron railing of the stairway.

A smug expression of victory flashed across the MERGE thug's face.

"Now I will kill you."

Mack Bolan's

PHOENIX FORCE

#1 Argentine Deadline
#2 Guerilla Games
#3 Atlantic Scramble
#4 Tigers of Justice
#5 The Fury Bombs
#6 White Hell
#7 Dragon's Kill
#8 Aswan Hellbox
#9 Ultimate Terror
#10 Korean Killground
#11 Return to Armageddon
#12 The Black Alchemists
#13 Harvest Hell
#14 Phoenix in Flames
#15 The Viper Factor
#16 No Rules, No Referee
#17 Welcome to the Feast
#18 Night of the Thuggee
#19 Sea of Savages
#20 Tooth and Claw
#21 The Twisted Cross
#22 Time Bomb
#23 Chip Off the Bloc

PHOENIX FORCE

Chip Off the Bloc

Gar Wilson

A GOLD EAGLE BOOK FROM
WORLDWIDE

TORONTO • NEW YORK • LONDON • PARIS
AMSTERDAM • STOCKHOLM • HAMBURG
ATHENS • MILAN • TOKYO • SYDNEY

First edition May 1986

ISBN 0-373-61323-7

Special thanks and acknowledgment to Paul Glen Neuman
for his contribution to this work.

Printed in Canada

1

It was a short vacation.

Monday was Disneyland. For eight hours, the three men enjoyed all that the Magic Kingdom had to offer: never-ending crowds, long lines and sore feet.

Tuesday they made the trek to Knott's Berry Farm and the Movieland Wax Museum. At Knott's, they panned for gold and then, after gorging themselves on fried chicken, the men drove up the street and had their pictures taken with John Wayne.

Wednesday was the boat ride to Catalina. Kirill Blinov and Sergei Kaplenko were seasick during the voyage to the island. On the way back to the mainland, it was Yuri Solotrin's turn. It was the first night they did not dine on American junk food.

Thursday they toured Universal Studios. By the end of the day, each of the three men were wearing Foster Grant sunglasses, and they had purchased more postcards than they had friends.

Friday their vacation ended. After checking out of their hotel, they took a taxi to a nearby used car dealership. They made their choice and bought a late model van with cash.

Catching the Hollywood Freeway in Burbank, they followed it north until it joined Interstate 5. Forty miles outside of Los Angeles and only a half hour from their ultimate destination, they stopped at a motel and rented a room.

The three men slept until eight and then drove to a fish-and-chips stand.

"Fantastic meal!" Kirill Blinov decided as he swallowed the last bite of battered cod. "It's the first fish I've had in years that didn't taste like old shoe leather."

Blinov held up the cardboard container and read aloud the slogan printed on top of the box. "A Whale of a Meal...At a Shrimp of a Price!" He smacked his lips, then reverted once more to his native Russian. "Why can't we get fish like this back home?"

Yuri Solotrin, sitting behind the wheel of the van, laughed at the question. "We don't get food like this in Moscow for the same reason most of what we've seen and done these past few days does not exist in the eyes of the Kremlin or, for that matter, in the eyes of the majority of our fellow countrymen. The Kremlin believes such a life-style would be decadent for the masses to endure."

"Yuri's right," agreed Sergei Kaplenko. "If a restaurant catering to the masses dared to serve a meal fit for human consumption instead of the slop they traditionally prepare, there would be riots every night as people tried to get a table."

"Exactly. And I would be the first in line," Blinov stated.

"Yes, well don't let Major Kulik hear you spouting such sentiments, or this will be the last time you are privileged to visit this country," warned Kaplenko.

"What Major Kulik doesn't know won't hurt us," Blinov protested. "Besides, our orders were to play the role of typical tourists visiting Los Angeles for the first time. We have only been obeying our instructions." He slurped the last of his chocolate milk shake, then crushed the paper cup in his fist. "Let's get this over with. There is a motion picture on television later to-night that I would like to see."

"What is the name of the film?" questioned Solo-trin.

"Does it make any difference, Comrade?" Blinov returned. "Whatever the movie is, you know we will not have seen it."

"Enough talk. Start the engine," Kaplenko or-dered. "It is time to go to work. The major is expect-ing us to make our delivery by ten."

"And the major will not be disappointed," Solo-trin promised.

The three men threw their trash out of the van's windows onto the ground. At that moment, they had more important things on their minds than whether or not they should litter American soil.

Yuri Solotrin started the engine and turned on the headlights. He dropped the transmission into Drive and then headed the van toward the tiny rural town of Piru.

The August night was warm and clear. Twilight faded in the west, while a full harvest moon shone brightly. The evening air was dry and scented with dust and vegetation.

They drove through Piru and past a grocery store whose dimly lit Food-Beer-Ammo sign kept flicker-ing on and off. A barking dog chased them for half a block before finally giving up. They continued to drive farther into the hills overlooking the rural community. A mile outside of Piru, Solotrin slowed the car and turned onto a private drive marked with a wagon wheel.

Solotrin promptly killed the headlights; the moon was high enough now to make them unnecessary. As the car crept down the drive, Blinov opened the glove compartment and took out a pair of handguns, passing an H&K P7 9 mm pistol back to Kaplenko and keeping an S&W Model 60 .38 Chief's Special stainless revolver for himself. Solotrin carried a Benelli 9 mm automatic in the pocket of his lightweight summer jacket.

"All systems are go." Solotrin stroked the exterior of his metal-filled pocket. "This is it."

They rounded a curve and caught the first sight of their target's home. It was a two-story house bordered by a row of hedges. A double garage was off to the right. The driveway bent in a U-shape in front of the house before doubling back on itself.

Solotrin was pleased with what he saw. He goosed the accelerator, shifted to Neutral and then shut off the engine. The van coasted the rest of the way up the drive, coming to a noiseless stop before their target's front door.

"We won't be long," Blinov said as he and Kaplenko, their weapons drawn, jumped from the van and moved toward the house.

Solotrin watched as Blinov tested the front door and found it unlocked. Kaplenko nudged the door open, and the two men disappeared inside. Solotrin settled back in his seat to wait.

A quick check aided by the moonlight streaming through the side windows showed the first floor of the house was deserted. The two men quickly advanced to the carpeted steps leading to the second floor.

Halfway up the stairs, they heard music. Kaplenko smiled as he recognized the piece—*Romeo and Juliet* by Tchaikovsky. It was one of his favorites.

The two men were lured in the direction of Tchaikovsky's famous melody. They came to an open doorway, glanced inside and found their target. He was working at a desktop computer in the far corner of the room. His back was to the Russians.

Just within the doorway was the compact disk player. Blinov crept into the room, then signaled to his partner, who responded by switching off the music. Sudden stillness filled the air.

"What?" The target pushed himself away from his desk as he swiveled around in his chair. His eyes widened in shock as he saw the strangers and their guns. "Who—" The target's voice cracked. "I mean, who the hell are you? What do you want?"

The target started to rise from his seat, but thought better of it when Blinov stepped forward. The Russian agent waved his Smith and Wesson menacingly as he stared at the man at the computer. "You are Robert Pearce?"

The target gulped. "I am Robert Pearce, yes. Look, if it's money you men want, I'm afraid you're out of luck. I never keep more than fifty dollars in cash here at—"

"Silence!" Sergei Kaplenko ordered as he moved further into the room. "Now that you have told us who you are, you have my permission to stand."

Pearce remained rooted in his chair. "Are you going to shoot me? Is that it?"

"Don't be ridiculous," Kirill Blinov scolded. "If we planned to shoot you, Mr. Pearce, you would already be dead. Now, do as you were told. Get out of the chair."

Pearce was visibly shaken, yet he managed to make his trembling legs support his weight. "And now?"

"Simple," Blinov explained. "You will accompany us downstairs and through the front door. We have a van parked in front of your house. We will take a short ride together. Understood?"

"While we don't wish to harm you, Mr. Pearce, you must be aware that the guns my associate and I are holding are not toys," added Kaplenko. "If you try to escape, I can assure you that you will be shot." He paused. "Well?"

Pearce's shoulders slumped in defeat. "It would appear that I don't have any choice."

"Believe us," Blinov said, "you don't. Shall we?" He stepped aside and motioned Pearce forward with his S&W Model 60. "It's getting late. You will walk between us. My associate will lead the way."

Pearce grumbled that he would do as instructed, and then glumly followed Kaplenko downstairs and out of the house.

As they moved toward the van, Kaplenko shook his head in surprise. Unbelievably, Solotrin appeared to have fallen asleep at the wheel of the van. Good friend or not, the comrade's careless attitude in the line of duty could not go unreported. Major Kulik would have to be told as soon as Robert Pearce was safely delivered.

Kaplenko crossed to the open window of the driver's side.

"Are you out of your mind, Yuri?" Kaplenko shook his slumbering friend by the shoulder. "How could you sleep at a—"

But then Solotrin's body rolled forward and bounced off the van's steering wheel so that his head rested against the door. Bright moonlight washed the Russian's face. Kaplenko gasped and backed away. Solotrin's throat had been slit, and blood continued to gurgle from the open wound.

"Sergei!" Kirill practically shouted. "What happened to Yuri?"

But before Sergei could reply, a male voice called from the direction of the hedges in front of the house.

"¡Buenas noches, mis amigos!"

Sergei Kaplenko spun toward the sound of the voice as a stuttering, coughing noise erupted around him. A volcano of pain burned across his belly. A stream of bullets stitched him open from sternum to groin. He tried to bring his H&K P7 into play, but before Kaplenko could fire a single shot, he collapsed and drowned in the instant tide of blood spilling from his waist.

Kirill Blinov did not fare any better. Watching as his comrade was butchered before his eyes, the dumbstruck Blinov was still staring at his friend's corpse when a triple burst of lead cracked open his skull in a spouting geyser of blood and bone fragments. The dead man's useless S&W raced his body to the ground.

Robert Pearce closed his eyes, expecting to share the same fate as his abductors. But when the pain did not come, he opened his eyes just as his saviors emerged from behind the hedges.

There were four men, three Hispanics and a powerfully built black man. All four carried submachine guns. The apparent leader of the group, a short Hispanic with a pencil-thin mustache, lowered his weapon and smiled at Pearce.

"Ah, Senor Pearce," the man said, his English bearing a heavy Spanish accent. "You are unharmed, no?"

Pearce took a deep breath and shuddered. "I am fine, yes."

"I am relieved to hear that, my friend," the leader of the four strangers confessed. "It is most fortunate that we happened to come along when we did. Most fortunate, indeed."

"You can say that again!" Pearce wiped his face with the back of his hand. "You and your men are responsible for saving my life tonight. I don't know how I can ever repay you."

The mysterious gunman laughed and handed his weapon to one of his friends as he took a small, black leather case from his pocket. He unzipped the case and removed a hypodermic syringe.

"Don't worry about repaying us for rescuing you," the man advised as he stepped forward. "I'm sure we'll think of something, Senor Pearce."

2

Sentry traveled quietly over the bumpy terrain, its computerized tread system allowing it to smoothly traverse any obstructions encountered along its route. A video camera mounted on Sentry's forward armament area scanned quickly from left to right, searching for intruders. An auxiliary camera kept watch from Sentry's rear.

Heat and motion sensors located deep within Sentry's logic core detected nothing unusual. A rabbit scurried across the viewfinder of its forward camera, but Sentry's internal identification photographic file instantly rated the small, furry creature as nonthreatening. Consequently, the rabbit was not killed.

A prototype Autonomous Land Vehicle or ALV, developed for the United States Army by the Defense Advanced Research Projects Agency, Sentry was enjoying, as much as it was capable of enjoying, one of its first field tests. DARPA, the research and development arm of the Department of Defense, was responsible for the development of all Artificial Intelligence and robotics projects for each of the three branches of the U.S. armed forces.

Sentry represented one of the first ALVs out of the cradle, the product of a marriage of microchip and steel that DARPA hoped would play an integral part in the Army's future. But in order for research on the ALV project to advance, Sentry had to be put through a battery of tests. The vehicle worked in theory, but it remained to be seen if it would really work in practice.

DARPA wanted Sentry's evaluation to be more than a simulated exercise wherein one computer pitted its programmed capabilities against another's. The DoD honchos wanted Sentry's test-bed phase to be more than a high-tech extension of a video arcade game. DARPA wanted Sentry to experience a confrontation with the finest combatants that the department could find.

The combatants DARPA wanted had a name: PHOENIX FORCE.

The five commandos belonging to the world's foremost fighting unit observed Sentry's progress from a quarter mile away. Hidden within a thicket of trees, the men of Phoenix Force were safe from Sentry's cameras and beyond the range of the ALV's ultrasensitive external sensors. As the five commandos scrutinized its actions, Sentry handily maneuvered itself up and over a fallen log that blocked its path. But not all of the Phoenix Force members were impressed.

"So much for the old butcher's hook, mates," David McCarter announced, keeping his voice to a low whisper. "With apologies to Karl," the Cockney counterterrorist indicated the man kneeling to his right, "Sentry is living proof that Volkswagen never stopped making the Bug. And that little piece of machinery's supposed to prevent the five of us from reaching our objective? Rubbish!"

Schooled in the tough-as-nails neighborhoods of London's East End, McCarter's talents in the battlefield had proved the critical difference between success and failure during numerous Phoenix Force missions. A veteran of the British Army where he excelled in foreign languages and every flying course available, the fox-faced Briton was also a superb pistol marksman.

Inevitably, McCarter's particular skills brought him to the attention of Britain's Special Air Service. The SAS gave him the chance to spread his wings, and it was while pulling duty with that elite group that McCarter saw action in Oman, Hong Kong and Northern Ireland, culminating in his participation in Operation Nimrod, the SAS raid on the Iranian Embassy in London.

Described at various times as courageous, impetuous and short-tempered, McCarter had also earned the reputation of being a hell of a scrapper when the going got tough. More often than not, McCarter's days and nights were spent with his life on the line. And that was exactly how he liked it.

"Sentry's little more than a glorified tin can," McCarter summed up his estimation of the advancing ALV.

"Yeah," Gary Manning felt obliged to point out, "well that *tin can* is packing enough punch to take on an army. Sentry's standard bag of tricks includes a couple of three-barreled 30 mm machine guns that spit out trouble at up to 2,000 RPM. The ALV's also equipped with a flamethrower and can deliver TOW-2 missiles postage free. The only reason DARPA held back on the TOWs is because the Department of Defense wanted to give us a fighting chance to come out of this test today in one piece."

Gary Manning had served in the Canadian Armed Forces, where a specialization in explosives led him to become one of the globe's top demolitions experts. His stint in the military included a tour in Vietnam with the 5th Special Forces and the clandestine Special Operations.

Manning was also an expert sniper who often selected a rifle over a handgun when it became his choice. The years spent honing his sniper skills explained why he was the best rifleman on the Phoenix Force team.

After Vietnam, Manning joined the Royal Canadian Mounted Police and quickly earned a position in their antiterrorist division. He had plenty to keep him busy, especially when the RCMP loaned him to West Germany's crack GSG-9 antiterrorist squad.

When the RCMP pulled out of the espionage trade, the newly formed Canadian Security Intelligence Service offered Manning the opportunity to trade in his cloak and dagger for a placid and safe career behind a desk. The CSIS would have had better luck convincing the man in the moon to grow a beard.

A civilian for the first time in years, Manning decided to seek work in the private sector, marry and raise a family. The marital union lasted just long enough for the ink to dry on his marriage certificate, but Manning took it all in stride. He excelled in business as a security consultant and soon found himself a junior executive for North America International, a position he was holding when chosen as one of the original members of Phoenix Force.

Manning kept his voice low as he continued to argue with McCarter. "Getting past Sentry is going to be a whole lot harder than you think."

"Ha!" McCarter smiled. "We'll see." He nodded to the lanky black American directly across from him. "Right, Calvin?"

The black man shrugged. "I make a habit of never underestimating any vehicle that doesn't have hubcaps."

The Briton's smile changed to a frown. "I knew I could depend on you."

Now it was James's turn to grin. "Sorry, man. Rules is rules."

Born and raised on Chicago's rough South Side, Calvin James learned early that the key to urban survival was a combination of quick thinking and fast fists. Hardworking and hard fighting, young James was a natural survivor.

He knew instinctively that life had to offer more than what he saw in the dilapidated tenements of his neighborhood. There had to be more to it than trying to get by on handouts and food stamps. Miracles were the stuff of fiction; no one was going to come along and snap his fingers and make everything right. James knew he would have to take his destiny into his own hands.

At seventeen, the youth from Chicago enlisted in the Navy where his training and experience as a hospital corpsman eventually led to his recruitment by the SEALs. A twenty-four-month tour in Vietnam ended abruptly after he was wounded during a hush-hush mission for Special Ops. His courage saw him decorated for valor and honorably discharged.

Fresh out of the service, James's hopes were high for a promising future. He had a profession he could be proud of, and he was determined to use his skills to elevate his family out of the poverty they had always known.

But Fate had other plans.

One personal tragedy after another, including the murders of his mother and sister, made James think hard about his own future. Although he was studying medicine and chemistry at UCLA at the time, James reevaluated his priorities and switched his area of concentration to the police sciences. An honors student at graduation, James traveled north and joined the San Francisco Police Department.

James was with the SFPD's SWAT team when elected by Phoenix Force to participate in what was intended to be a solo mission. That job turned full-time after Keio Ohara, one of the Phoenix team's founding members, fell in combat on the very same assignment.

While James may have been the youngest commando to join the Force's ranks, his years of experience made him every bit as important as any other man on the team. When asked to give one hundred percent, James always managed one hundred and ten.

"I'm afraid I've got to run with Manning on this one, David," James apologized to his British friend. "Sentry's definitely going to be a formidable cookie to crumble."

McCarter shrugged, then turned to his right. "What about you, Karl? When it comes to microchipped monstrosities like Sentry, you know more than all of us put together. Has DARPA come up with a substitute for a flesh and blood soldier?"

"A substitute? No," Hahn replied. "Sentry, in its present incarnation, can only be classified as an AI-robotic alternative to having a human patrolling a known parameter. Sentry can only function as well as its programming enables it to."

Karl Hahn had initially worked with Phoenix Force during their battle to destroy a mad KGB scheme launched in Istanbul. Hahn was an agent with the West German BND, that country's federal intelligence service, and had spent a total of eight years stationed in Turkey.

A former member of GSG-9, Hahn had played a part in several key strikes against the Baader-Meinhof gang and the German Red Army as well as Turkish terrorists operating in West Berlin. His transfer to the BND came about because of his habit of hunting down and killing Red Army fanatics on his own—a vendetta that began after a friend in the GSG-9 was tortured, castrated and blinded by the modern-day savages.

Fluent in German, English and Turkish and with a working knowledge of Czech, Russian and French, Hahn majored in computer programming at UCLA after attending high school in Southern California. He was also an electronics wizard and an expert in weapons design.

Hahn's present association with Phoenix Force stemmed from the potentially tragic consequences of a Force attack on the ODESSA Nazi stronghold of Pic d'Esteve, high in the Pyrenees mountains of southern France. During the final assault on the Nazi fortress, another of the Phoenix squad's original members had fallen in combat.

This time, the victim of the never-ending war against those who would dominate the world with cruelty and terror was Rafael Encizo. The Cuban-born veteran of the Bay of Pigs invasion had dedicated his life to fighting for the rights of the oppressed everywhere. Encizo was slowly recuperating in a U.S. military hospital in Germany with the hope that one day he would be strong enough to rejoin Phoenix Force. Until that time, Hahn had bravely agreed to walk in Encizo's footsteps.

"So, what's all that boil down to?" McCarter asked the West German. "Is Sentry going to be a snap to take on or not?"

"My feeling," Hahn said, "is that even with the limitations of Sentry's AI capabilities, going one-on-one with the ALV will be similar to a female canine giving birth."

"You'd better explain that one," McCarter said.

"It's going to be a real bitch," Manning supplied.

"Right," confirmed Hahn.

"Your speculations will soon be academic, gentlemen," Yakov Katzenelenbogen, unit commander of Phoenix Force indicated. "Sentry is fast approaching."

Looking more like a college professor who had been teaching the same history course for twenty-five years, the Israeli colonel's slightly paunchy midsection, iron-gray hair and peaceful blue eyes all but hid the fact that Katzenelenbogen was one of the globe's most accomplished antiterrorists. If anything about the man betrayed the true nature of his chosen vocation, it was the fact that his right arm had been amputated just below the elbow.

Katz had devoted more than forty years of his life to combating injustice wherever it raised its ugly head. As a teen, he joined the Resistance movement and fought against Nazi oppression during World War II. Katz later became a member of the Haganah in aid of Israel's quest for independence from the British. Afterward, his aptitude for tackling impossible assignments grew when he joined the Mossad.

Katz overcame physical and emotional adversity to emerge stronger than before when he lost both his only son and his right arm in the Six Day War. A compassionate man whose fierce determination and wisdom had repeatedly been tested under the most trying of conditions, Colonel Katzenelenbogen had continually inspired the respect and trust of the men of Phoenix Force.

"You all know what's expected of us," Katz offered by way of a final word of encouragement. "Sentry stands between us and our objective, which is a designated supply depot that lies inside the area Sentry's programmed to protect. This depot, actually a strip of red cloth secured about the trunk of a tree, is approximately one half mile from our present position.

"Our goal is to reach the cloth strip and remove it from the tree. This will automatically trigger a response that disengages Sentry's armament capabilities. The DoD brass wanted to test Sentry against the best men available. I know we won't disappoint them."

Sentry was only a hundred yards away when Phoenix Force went into action. Carrying his S&W M-76 SMG tucked close to his body, James was the first of the five to break out into the open. He kept his head down low as he ran in a zigzag pattern for a nearby grove of trees.

As James dashed across the viewfinder of the ALV's forward camera, Sentry's internal photographic file immediately rated the fleeing figure as an intruder. Sentry doubled its overland speed and began rotating its twin, triple-barreled 30 mm machine guns in the enemy's direction. The percussion primed 30 mm ammunition could streak into a target with a muzzle velocity of twenty-two hundred feet per second. Sentry's sensors confirmed an easy kill.

James had yet to reach the second grove of trees when Sentry opened fire, its machine guns burning the air twenty-five feet behind the American's heels, angry bullets sweeping after him in a storm of destruction. James dove for the ground. The 30 mms missed him by inches and vented their wrath on the trees he had been running for.

The black Phoenix warrior shielded his face and forced himself deeper into the dirt. The noise from bullets plowing into wood sounded as though a crazed lumberjack were trying to chop down all the trees in the forest at the same time. The sound was not misleading.

When the shooting stopped abruptly, James uncovered his eyes and saw that the grove he was facing had been transformed into a mass of Texan-sized toothpicks. Severed tree limbs were everywhere, scattered upon the ground in a salad of needles and pine sap. Splinters and sawdust swirled in the air. Behind him, he could hear Sentry's powerful treads crunching over the earth toward him.

"Terrific," James moaned.

Manning sighted carefully down the scope of his H&K G3SG-1 rifle on the lens of the auxiliary video camera on Sentry's rear and fired. Even though the ALV was bouncing up and down in his sights as it charged after James, the Phoenix team's prime rifleman scored a direct hit. Manning confirmed as much through the scope of his Heckler and Koch.

Only something was wrong. Although the Canadian knew his aim had been true, the lens of Sentry's rear camera appeared to be intact. It had not even been scratched. Frustrated, Manning lined up his sights and fired once more, then again and again. The result was the same. Sentry kept rolling along like nothing had happened. It was almost as though Sentry were laughing at him.

Sentry *was* laughing, at least as much as its AI program enabled it to. The ALV's on-board computer had recorded a total of four shots striking the lens of its rear camera. Sentry's tactile sensors told the ALV that each round had been a 7.62 mm, far underpowered to do the auxiliary camera any damage. Its lens was protected by a microfine mesh alloy tempered to withstand much higher calibers.

Sentry made an instantaneous check of the intruder it had been chasing and found that he was positioned flat on the ground, not moving. Injured, perhaps? Sentry ran a thermal check on the intruder's body temperature. No, the man was not out of commission. The intruder only wanted Sentry to think so. Sentry was not so easily fooled.

Three more 7.62 mm rounds slammed into the lens of Sentry's rear camera. The ALV applied its brakes and came to a halt. Decisions. Decisions. Continue attacking the prone intruder or investigate the sniper? Another barrage of 7.62 mm fire made Sentry's decision easy.

James was about to get up when a deadly stream of flame arced overhead. Instinctively, he pancaked to the ground and rolled swiftly to the right. The flame splashed into the bullet-riddled grove of trees and whooshed into a roaring inferno. Intense heat threatened to engulf him in a fiery embrace as he leaped to his feet and ran.

Sentry was satisfied. The intruder who pretended to be injured could no longer move forward into Sentry's path. Good. This left Sentry free to deal with the sniper.

Manning had watched as Sentry stopped and tried to trap James in the burning spray of flame. It was a decent try, but no cigar. Then Manning quickly forgot about James and started worrying about his own well-being. And with good reason. The ALV suddenly lurched forward, performed a surprisingly tight U-turn and began speeding straight toward Manning's hiding spot.

Sentry knew where the sniper was concealed. When the lens of its rear camera was first struck, Sentry automatically performed a reverse trajectory analysis of the initial 7.62 mm round, effectively isolating the location of the gunman to within a radius of five feet. There could be no mistake. The sniper was lurking behind a clump of trees at the top of the low hill rising just ahead. The ALV's forward camera could not actually see the sniper, but Sentry's AI sensors were not alarmed.

The Canadian aimed and fired, each of the big bore H&K's rounds going where Manning wanted them to. But none of the sniping rifle's 7.62 mm projectiles phased Sentry in the least. The ALV kept coming. Manning swore as the G3's standard twenty-round magazine ran dry.

Katz and Hahn simultaneously blasted away at the advancing ALV; the Israeli put his Uzi through its paces while the BND specialist relied on an H&K MP-5A3 machine pistol. The two Phoenix commandos directed their gunfire toward opposite sides of the rapidly moving ALV.

Sparks danced over Sentry's polished surface as a 9 mm hell storm came out of nowhere. Sentry applied its brakes again to investigate this latest disturbance, its forward camera twisting back and forth on its metallic stalk. The camera showed more intruders wielding automatic weapons, but as with the sniper fire, Sentry was not overly concerned. The bullets striking its exostructure scarcely registered on its delicate tactile sensors. The bullets were harmless.

Sentry put its attack on the sniper on hold while it evaluated this latest development. Altogether, four intruders had violated territory Sentry was programmed to protect. Which of the intruders should be destroyed first?

Unlike problem solving performed by the human brain where more than a single aspect of a given situation can be dealt with at a given time, parallel processing of data was impossible for Sentry. Regardless of how incredibly swiftly its on-board computer might function, Sentry's AI-robotics limited the Autonomous Land Vehicle to sequential processing. The ALV could deal with only one task at a time.

Sentry's logic core ran through its options. Intruder number one had fled on foot to escape the burning trees and no longer posed an immediate threat. The sniper had ceased firing—another problem postponed. Intruders three and four were a nuisance more than anything else, their puny weapons doing no damage at all. Yet intruders three and four were closer than the others, making the pair tempting targets. With a top overland speed of forty miles per hour on a flat stretch of ground, Sentry concluded it would have little difficulty running or gunning down the intruders once they were flushed out into the open. But which one to start with?

Hahn helped make the decision by choosing that moment to launch a Mk II fragmentation grenade at Sentry. The Mk II rolled off the tips of the West German's fingers as he released the grenade with a snapping motion of his wrist. Packed with two ounces of flaked TNT, the grenade sailed through the air and touched down precisely in front of the ALV. Seconds later, the Mk II exploded with a roar.

Sentry's audio detectors whined in protest. Shrapnel and debris clouded the viewer of its forward camera. Its central processing unit ordered and received a damage report. The examination revealed the impossible. A quarter-inch scratch had been gouged on the idling wheel near the anterior left section of its tread.

A quarter-inch scratch now marred Sentry's otherwise flawless surface.

The ALV sensed an internal buildup of heat as its AI chips reacted to the damage.

Katz and Hahn watched as the machine revved its engine in a throbbing fever of noise. When it seemed as though its motor would shatter from the strain, Sentry released its brakes, lurching ahead, the abrupt transition from motionless to mobile lifting the front of the ALV off the ground. Gravity took over and Sentry's treads chewed into the earth, searching for traction and finding it. The ALV rushed uphill for fifty-five feet before turning to the left and racing at an angle straight for Hahn.

"Scheissen!" Hahn swore, the H&K MP-5A3 he held about as useful as a slingshot.

Sentry's engine churned even faster after its optics generator locked on to the intruder it sought. It would be simple to eliminate the invader using the flamethrower or 30 mm machine guns, but much too easy. Better to trample the interloper into the dirt, to crush the trespasser under its treads. Much better. Sentry was flawless no longer. Sentry had been scratched.

The ALV charged at Hahn, fully intending to run him down. Hahn stood at the end of a row of trees beneath a canopy of branches. Sentry was almost upon him.

McCarter's timing was perfect. Waiting until just before Sentry passed below the branch on which he crouched, the Briton dropped from his perch and landed atop the speeding ALV. The Phoenix commando clamped his hands around the metal stalk that jutted up from Sentry like a unicorn's horn. He interlaced his fingers over the lens of the camera mounted on the stalk.

Denied a view of where it was going, Sentry's sensors defensively locked its treads, throwing the ALV into a slide. Hahn barely had time to dive out of the way before Sentry slammed full force into the row of trees.

The impact of the violent collision caused McCarter to lose his balance. Only the fact that he was able to grip the camera prevented him from sailing through space. As McCarter worked to regain his balance, Sentry's treads spun furiously in reverse.

The ALV pulled away from the trees, utilizing its auxiliary camera at the rear for guidance while it backed out of the intruder's ambush. Clearly, Sentry deducted, the total number of invaders was five. Not four. Also understood was the priority in which the intruders should be disposed of. The one clinging to and obscuring the lens of Sentry's forward camera had to go first.

Twice McCarter thought his ride was finished as Sentry attempted to shake him loose. Only the Briton's strength and tenacious grip saved him. Even so, he knew Sentry's tactics would eventually win out. As long as the ALV's auxiliary camera was functional, Sentry called the shots. It could storm over the countryside until its fuel supply was exhausted.

Sentry became fully operable again when the optical sensors of its forward camera suddenly began to work. This AI-robotic version of euphoria lasted only as long as it took a quick-thinking McCarter to strip off his field jacket and drape it over top of the ALV's camera. He secured the jacket in place by tying the sleeves together and then dove for the back of the ALV and its second camera. The instant McCarter's hands closed over the front of his objective, Sentry rocked to a bone-jarring halt. The British commando had expected this reaction and had braced himself accordingly. When the rocking motion of the gradually settling Sentry stopped, McCarter was still a passenger.

"Having fun?" Manning asked from McCarter's left.

The Cockney swiveled his head toward the Canadian. "A right bash, thanks. Give me your jacket so I can cover this camera like I did the other."

Manning stepped over and did as requested. Once the sleeves of the coat were knotted to his satisfaction, the Englishman slid off the rear of the ALV onto the ground. Sentry's engine idled for a moment, then a tremor rumbled through the vehicle and its motor died.

"Some glorified tin can," Manning reminded McCarter of his initial assessment of Sentry. "Now what do you have to say about it?"

The Briton responded by kicking Sentry in its side. "Where do they keep the batteries?"

The Canadian had no time to reply as Hahn and James appeared from opposite directions. Hahn was wiping dirt and pine needles from his jacket. James carried the strip of red cloth in his hands. By reaching and untying the piece of material from around the tree, James had been responsible for the shutdown of Sentry's engine and defenses.

"That's all of us but Katz," James commented, approaching the group at a comfortable run. "Anybody seen him?"

"Right here," the Israeli colonel answered for himself, entering the clearing by pushing out from behind a dense clump of vegetation. The expression on Katzenelenbogen's face left no doubt that something was wrong.

"What's the good word?" Manning asked.

Katz touched his left hand to the miniature two-way radio hanging from his belt. "I just finished speaking with Hal. A chopper's on its way to pick up up. It's flying us directly to Stony Man."

"Sounds serious," James said. "Did Hal indicate what's up?"

Katz nodded. "I wish he hadn't."

3

Hal Brognola torched off a cigar, his third in a row, and began filling the conference room with yet another layer of smoke. At the moment, he was nervous. As the nation's top Federal agent, he had a right to be. He planted the cheroot in the corner of his mouth and lightly drummed his fingers across the top of his desk.

Phoenix Force was due any minute. Soon his Stony Man supercrew would be asked to unselfishly risk their lives in order to make the best of a bad situation. Brognola did not doubt that all of the five would willingly answer the call to duty. They had stormed the hell grounds before. They would do so again. The men of Phoenix Force were a special breed of soldier: they were five who fought like five hundred. Brognola was damn proud to work with them.

Sending Phoenix Force out to confront the scum of each new mission was never easy. In the back of his mind, Brognola was always painfully aware that *this* assignment could prove to be the last for one or all of his men. With Keio Ohara honored by a small gravestone in Arlington Cemetery and Rafael Encizo recovering from a head wound that had almost killed him, the realities of the dangers that came with membership to Stony Man were never far from home.

Stony Man was conceived as a base for waging war against international terrorism. The operation had been jointly founded by Hal Brognola and a close personal friend. That friend was Mack Bolan, known to the world at large as the Executioner.

For too many years, the legions of jackals called terrorists had gorged themselves on a steady diet of hate and fear. Aided by technological advances and sophisticated weaponry, the terrormongers had grown bold inflicting their twisted ideals on innocents. With little danger of reprisal, the courageous murderers of the defenseless had multiplied and spread their diseased philosophy unchecked.

Like the surgeon who knows that certain tools of the trade are required to remove a malignant tumor without destroying other parts of the body, the Stony Man personnel realized they would never cure the epidemic by carving away at the cancer of terrorism through civilized negotiations. Bargaining with wild animals was impossible. It was much better to speak to the beasts in a language they understood.

Brognola's expression lost some of its tension as the men he had been waiting for noisily entered the conference room.

"Cor!" McCarter announced as he waved his hands back and forth in front of his face. "Somebody call the fire brigade." The Briton took a seat, then said to Brognola, "How many cigars in a row, Hal?"

Brognola held up three fingers.

"No wonder it's like a smokehouse in here," James observed. "Three King Edwards in a row, though?"

The American commando sat down. "Whatever's cooking on the stove must be pretty damn awful."

"It is," the nation's number-one Fed confirmed as the rest of the team found chairs.

"We knew you wouldn't airlift us from the DARPA proving grounds unless it was an emergency," Manning said. "And the only information Katz could give us was that it involved a critical breach of national security."

Brognola nodded. "I didn't elaborate over the radio because I felt it best if all of you were briefed on the situation at the same time."

"Fire away, Hal." Katz, who hated to fly, popped an antacid into his mouth. "What have you got for us?"

"A little over an hour ago, the President received some distressing news," Brognola began. "Are any of you familiar with a man by the name of Robert Pearce?"

"I believe I've run across his name through business dealings at North America International," Manning offered. "Isn't he some hotshot scientist under contract to the U.S. government?"

"If he's who I think he is," Hahn added, "then he's much more than a scientist. The Robert Pearce I've heard of has written a brilliant series of articles on advanced computer programming techniques. Is that our man?"

"Yes," Brognola confirmed. "For the past twenty-seven months, Robert Pearce has been working on a project closely linked with the American Strategic Defense Initiative."

"Star Wars?" James asked. "What kind of link are you talking about?"

"Tighter than the ones on the fence around Fort Knox," the Fed returned. "Most of you probably know that one of the primary criticisms against fully funding a defense program of the magnitude of the SDI operation is that present technology will not permit the Star Wars package to viably serve its intended purpose for at least another twenty years.

"Other negative views give the project the thumbs-down because, even if the funding is made available, there's no real guarantee that the SDI equipment will work once it is finally launched into space."

"It wouldn't be the first time a DoD golden goose turned out to be a turkey," James said.

McCarter pulled a Players cigarette from the pack in his breast pocket. "And this Pearce guy has developed a method for overcoming some of the gripes against getting the show on the road?" He lit his smoke. "Is that it?"

"Exactly," Brognola replied. "Without going into the technical specifics, the project Robert Pearce has been a part of for more than two years now effectively bypasses many of the difficulties the SDI was expected to encounter. The innovative computer programming process he's helped develop shows every sign of utilizing current technology to significantly advance the American debut of the so-called Star Wars program."

"What kind of jump in the schedule are we talking about here?" Katz asked.

"Conservative estimates suggest that the research Pearce is doing could feasibly result in the launch of an operable SDI prototype into space in just under a decade."

Manning whistled. "Less than half of the predicted time. The guy must be one hell of a programmer. His importance to the success of the SDI must be incredible."

"Which is why the President was notified as soon as it was learned that Robert Pearce had vanished," Brognola said. "He disappeared from his house in southern California last night some time between ten and midnight."

"Disappeared?" Hahn mused. "Don't tell me the President is worried Robert Pearce may have defected. I haven't met the man, but from the tone of his articles, I don't think he's a traitor."

"And he isn't suspected of being one," the Fed assured the West German. "Even if that were a consideration, you can throw all thoughts about Robert Pearce getting up on the the Red side of the bed right out the window. Three bodies that we have since identified as KGB operatives were discovered murdered at the Pearce home early this morning. They were found by a neighbor who came over to return a lawn mower he had borrowed. He phoned the police and the matter soon came to the attention of the President. That's when he called me."

Brognola served as the liaison between Stony Man and the Oval Office. The President was the only one in the White House who knew Stony Man existed. Even so, the commander in chief was told only what Hal Brognola felt he should know.

"Three dead KGB agents," Manning said. "How were they killed, Hal?"

"One had his throat slashed; the other two were shot to death. Whoever iced them was playing for keeps. All of the Soviets were armed. Their weapons were still on the scene when the police arrived and none had been fired."

"Any indication of a struggle as far as Pearce was concerned?" James questioned.

"According to the authorities in California, no. For all they know, Pearce might not have been there when the three KGB agents were put away."

"Somehow, I doubt that," Katz suggested. "The Soviets weren't liquidated for peeking through the windows. My guess says they were probably killed because they were trying to bag Pearce."

"Something along the lines of a snatch and scratch?" Brognola asked.

"No," the Israeli countered. "From what you've told us, Robert Pearce would be more valuable to the Kremlin alive than dead, but only if he were alive and living in Moscow. That way, the Russians could drain his brain and put that knowledge to use on their own SDI program."

"But how can that be?" Manning wondered sarcastically. "The peace-loving Soviets have assured us they have no interest at all in developing a Star Wars operation of their own."

"Ha, ha, ha." McCarter's laughter was as flat as a glass of day-old champagne. "That's the same dodgy crap they came up with to try and get the U.S. to back off on its antisatellite weapons system. No small surprise there. The Soviets have been cultivating their own vastly inferior ANSAT setup for the past twenty years. They never have been keen on competition."

"Okay," James said. "Then maybe it was like Katz was saying. Perhaps the KGB trio stopped by Pearce's house to take him on a late-night ride." He looked to Brognola. "Were the Soviets killed inside or outside the house?"

"Outside," replied the Fed.

"It fits then," James continued. "The Russians could have already had Pearce in their possession when they were hit, probably just as they took Pearce out the front door. Did the Soviets have a vehicle parked on the premises, Hal?"

"A van purchased earlier in the day from a used car dealership in Hollywood. The KGB operative with the air-conditioned throat was found behind the wheel of the van."

"That fits, too," James went on. "If the Soviets left one of their men outside to keep watch, and things went fairly smoothly once they got to Pearce, then the other two KGB agents would have been pretty confident that everything was going according to plan when they started back to the van with their prize. Obviously, since none of the Russians managed to fire their weapons, they weren't expecting trouble and were caught by surprise."

"And whoever surprised them," Hahn said, following James's line of thinking, "is the party who now has Pearce. Have any ransom demands been made?"

"None so far," Brognola answered. "Whoever has Robert Pearce under wraps is keeping damn quiet about it. The California authorities are maintaining a low profile on the kidnapping from their end, too. So far, the media has been kept in the dark."

"Which is better for us," Manning indicated. "If we have to go out there and try and locate Pearce, the last thing we need is to have our faces featured coast-to-coast on the evening news."

"Exactly," Brognola agreed. "Which brings me to another problem. While we're reasonably certain that Robert Pearce is still alive, we're equally sure his captors may simply decide to kill him."

"If Pearce is such an integral part of the SDI program," McCarter said, "why on earth would they bump the guy off?"

Brognola sighed. "Because sooner or later, Pearce's abductors may discover they have the wrong man."

"What?" Katz leaned forward. "You mean Robert Pearce really isn't who everybody thinks he is?"

"Oh, he's tied in with the SDI operation, all right," Brognola resounded. "But the real breakthroughs for the SDI advances haven't come from Pearce."

"Who then?" Hahn sounded genuinely astonished.

"Pearce's son, Robert Jr."

"His son?" Manning repeated. "How old is he?"

"Bobby Pearce will be fourteen on his next birthday."

"That's great," James said. "So what you're telling us is that this Bobby kid, and not his dad, is the smarts behind putting the U.S. Star Wars program more than a decade ahead?"

Hal Brognola nodded. "Correct. Virtually all of the articles on advanced computer programming techniques that Karl mentioned he's read were, in fact, written by Bobby Pearce, not his father. The boy's a genius."

"Then why keep it a secret?" Hahn questioned.

"To protect the integrity of the SDI operation," Brognola told him. "It's estimated that expenditures for fully implementing SDI could run as high as one hundred billion dollars. Funding to get the ball rolling has not been easy to come by. If word leaked out that a crucial portion of SDI's success hinged on the work of a thirteen-year-old, the research and development money for Star Wars would evaporate overnight. Only a handful of top-ranking individuals within the government know the truth."

"Where was Bobby Pearce when his father was abducted?" asked James.

"Fortunately, for him and for us," Brognola said, "Bobby Pearce was attending classes at the Albert Risson Computer Camp that is located in the Angeles National Forest."

"Computer camp?" McCarter said. "What's he doing there... brushing up on his RAM and ROM?"

"Bobby Pearce is one of the instructors."

The British commando grumbled, "Oh."

"I'm sending the five of you to California at once," Brognola informed Phoenix Force. "Once you arrive, Katz, you and Gary go to the Pearce home and check for any clues the local authorities may have missed."

"And the rest of us?" James wanted to know.

"I want you, David and Karl out to the Albert Risson Computer Camp. Bobby Pearce has not been informed that his dad has been kidnapped. I'll leave it up to you to tell him. And then, I want you to take Bobby Pearce into protective custody."

"Baby-sit, you mean," McCarter corrected.

"Whatever you like." Brognola shrugged. "Just see to it that the cruds who killed the three KGB agents and then kidnapped his father don't get the boy."

4

The elephants upstairs were wearing boots and dancing.

Robert Pearce groaned and opened his eyes to the shadowy interior of a room. He was on a bed with his aching head resting upon a foam pillow. The pachyderms doing the stomp inside his skull danced harder. He winced and tiny red-and-green lights exploded across his eyes. His stomach jumped and he thought he would be sick.

A cool, white sheet was draped over his body. Beneath the light covering, he was fully clothed. He inhaled deeply and tried to sit up, but he was far too weak to do so.

His bed was the only piece of furniture in the room. There was a glass globe suspended from the ceiling. A narrow window was opposite the end of the bed. The cream-colored shade kept out most of the sunlight.

His mind digested the fact that it was sunny outside, and that told him he had been unconscious for many hours, perhaps days. He opened his mouth and licked his lips with the dry cotton wad of his tongue. Rubbing his mouth with sandpaper could not have been worse.

He did not remember much. He had been working in his study when two strangers barged in and then marched him downstairs and out the front door at gunpoint. It was a numbing experience, like it was happening to somebody else, not really to him.

Outside, they were walking toward a van when a voice called out from behind. Then there were gunshots and the two men abducting him were dead. After that, relief that quickly disappeared when it dawned on him that his rescuers had merely saved him for themselves.

Hands reached for him from the darkness and held him tight. A sudden sharp pain jabbed his left arm, and then he was sinking down into a slow-spinning tunnel of swirling black. And that was where his memory died. Where he was now was anybody's guess, and that went double for what was going to happen to him. He was completely in the dark.

Voices moving in the hallway outside his room drifted from one side of his door to the other. Then the voices were gone and he was alone again. He listened carefully for any additional sounds that might help to identify his whereabouts, but there was nothing. The unfamiliar building had grown silent.

The elephants in his head took a well deserved break, and Pearce focused his eyes on the shade that covered the window. Behind the shade, he could see the silhouette of crisscrossed metal bars. This was no ordinary room. It was more like a jail cell.

He heard the voices again, but this time they did not go away when they reached his room. The door was unlocked and, a few seconds later, the globe hanging from the ceiling was full of light. Pearce was still blinking his eyes against the unaccustomed brightness when he recognized a male voice.

"Ah, Senor Pearce. I am so pleased to see you have awakened from your sleep. Did you have a nice rest?"

Robert Pearce squinted at the figure standing next to the bed. It was the short Hispanic with the pencil-thin mustache—the same man he remembered coming at him with a hypodermic needle. Only now the man was unarmed and, instead of a syringe full of drugs, the stranger held a glass of water in his hands.

Pearce opened his mouth to speak, but his tongue would not cooperate. A rasping noise from the back of his throat was all he could manage. He raised a hand and gestured to the water glass.

"That is exactly why I decided to check on you, my friend. I thought you might be thirsty."

The man handed Pearce the glass and waited for him to drink every drop. Pearce passed the empty glass back to his captor.

"Very good," the Hispanic said, taking the glass. "Much better. See? I'll give you some more in a few minutes if you like, but first I think we should get acquainted."

Pearce swallowed his last mouthful of water and washed much of the gritty taste away. He made another attempt to speak, and this time his tongue cooperated.

"Who are you?" Pearce questioned. "Where am I? Why have you brought me here?"

"Please, Senor Pearce," the man protested, "please. One question at a time."

"Fine. Who are you?"

"You may call me your friend."

"Don't give me that!" Pearce said angrily. "I'm being held prisoner here against my will."

"What kind of gratitude is that for saving you from the men who broke into your house?"

"Forget it. Obviously, you and your associates were planning the same thing, or you wouldn't have been there to stop the others."

"I'm not going to insult your intelligence by denying it, but look on the bright side. If we hadn't been at your house last night, the chances are very good that you would be on your way to Moscow right now."

"I thought you weren't going to insult my intelligence?"

"We have every reason to suspect that the men leading you into the van were Soviet agents, possibly from the KGB."

Pearce paused. "That's crazy."

"There were three men participating in your abduction, not two."

"A third man was driving the van. I know."

"We quietly eliminated him before you and your escorts left the house, but before he expired, he swore at us by saying *pizdiuk*. You have heard the term before?"

Pearce shook his head.

"It is Russian for bastard."

"What about it?" Pearce remained unconvinced. "Many people speak Russian. That doesn't necessarily make them KGB agents."

"True, Senor Pearce, but they weren't exactly tourists, either, were they?"

"Forget about them. They're dead. I want to know why I'm here and what you intend to do with me?"

The Hispanic thoughtfully ran his fingers over his mustache. "I suppose you could say our intentions are along the lines shared by the Soviets."

"What am I? Some sort of political prisoner, then?"

The short Hispanic laughed. "The people I represent have no interest in political matters. We are much more interested in marketing. We provide goods and services for those who will pay for them, and right now, my friend, you are the featured item in this week's catalog. Your government will gladly spend whatever we ask for your safe return."

Pearce pulled away the sheet and slowly swung his feet to the floor. His head hurt like hell. The elephants were starting to dance again.

"Listen," Pearce said. "I hate to disappoint you, but the ransom you would get for me wouldn't buy dinner for four at a nice restaurant. You've made a mistake. I'm not as important as you think I am. I'm strictly small potatoes."

"Now it is you, Senor Pearce, who is insulting *my* intelligence. If we made a mistake, as you suggest, then it is the same error the Soviets were making. And how likely is that? Not very. We know enough about who you are and what you do for the American government to know that it will eagerly agree to pay us so that you may continue working on the Star Wars program.

"Of course, taking into account the recent amount of attention the Soviets have shown you gives us something else to consider. Who is to say? Perhaps Moscow will offer us more for you than Washington?"

"My earlier assessment of you stands, mister." Pearce did his best to sound tough. "You are crazy. And you can do what you want. You'll get no help from me."

"Maybe you will change your mind after we have had a chance to speak to your son."

At the mention of his boy, Pearce leaped off the bed to attack his captor.

"Why, you dirty—"

The Hispanic caught Pearce across the face with a vicious backhand that sent the man reeling back toward the bed.

"We'll have no more of that," the Hispanic ordered. "So long as you are here, you will do as you are told. Don't be stupid and make me hit you again. I don't like dealing in damaged merchandise."

Pearce ran his tongue over his bleeding lip. "You'll never get away with it."

Again, the short Hispanic laughed. "As far as you are concerned, Senor Pearce, we already have."

5

Not everyone enjoys hearing from the folks back home.

Carefully rereading the coded communiqué from his superiors in Moscow for the final time, Major Viktor Kulik would have preferred not to have heard from them at all. He scrunched the message into a tight ball that he threw into the bathroom sink. He doused the message with a generous squirt of cigarette lighter fluid, then dropped a lighted match into the basin. When the message was reduced to a mound of brittle ashes, he turned on the faucet and washed the mess down the drain.

Simply put, Kulik reflected as he dried the basin, the men calling the shots back home were pissed. And with good reason. The delicately orchestrated scheme to abduct the American computer wizard had failed miserably. Not only did the KGB not have Robert Pearce in its custody, but in attempting to kidnap Pearce, three top operatives had been lost. As the Los Angeles divisional control officer in charge of the abduction, the responsibility for failing to apprehend Pearce rested solely upon Kulik's shoulders.

The Collegium, Moscow's KGB leadership, was not overly keen on embarrassing surprises. Coming up with a suitable explanation for the American government as to why three sons of Mother Russia happened to end up dead at the home of a famous U.S. computer programmer was not exactly the kind of game the KGB enjoyed. Kulik knew from experience that when the shit hit the fan, someone always got splattered, and right now, the crap was headed his way.

The major left the can of lighter fluid by the sink and switched off the bathroom light. He then went into the living room of the rented house where he sat on a three-piece sectional sofa. Kulik glanced at the man who was already in the room with undisguised annoyance. As usual, Captain Oleg Lensky was glued to the television set, this time mindlessly watching a show about a bald policeman from New York who chased criminals as he sucked on a lollipop.

Kulik had seen plenty of stupid things in his fifty-eight years, but nothing as dumb as this. He reached for the remote control device on the coffee table and turned off the set.

"Hey, why did you do that?" Lensky complained immediately.

"We have more important business to occupy ourselves with than inane American television programs," Kulik replied. "I don't know why you insist on watching the shows, anyway. If you ask me, they are all the same."

"Not true," Lensky defended his viewing habits. "I have seen many shows in the two weeks we have been here, but I have yet to see a tractor or the appropriate farm implement starring in a lead role. I don't know how the Americans do it."

"Yes, well, get your mind off American television. As I said, you and I have more important matters on our plate."

"The news in the communiqué was not favorable, then?"

"An understatement if ever I've heard one. No, the news was not good. Our friends back home are not especially delighted with the recent turn of events."

"Ah," Lensky said, "those three bumblers were fools to get themselves killed. And without delivering Pearce to us! I told you we didn't need them for the job. We could have captured Pearce by ourselves. Isn't that what I said?"

"Yes," Kulik agreed, "but until you are in a position of authority and can be trusted to make policy decisions for the rest of us, then I am afraid you must learn to follow orders. Which, I suggest, is what we do. We are in enough hot water as it is."

Lensky suddenly jumped from the couch and began to pace. "So that's the way it's to be, is it? We are saddled with using Blinov, Kaplenko and Solotrin for the job, and when they fail to deliver the goods, then we are the ones held responsible. Bah, how I hate injustice!"

"Calm yourself!" the major ordered. "We may be in the stew, but it's not on the stove yet. There may, after all, be a way for us to salvage this business concerning Pearce."

"And how do we do that? Los Angeles is a big city, and not all of its animals are in the zoo. We don't have any idea where to begin to look for Pearce."

"That's easy. We will begin our search in the same place Blinov and his idiot companions misplaced the scientist."

"What?" Lensky's mouth fell open. "At Pearce's home?"

"Precisely."

"What good will that do? Pearce has already been taken. Whoever has him has no reason to go back to the house."

"We don't know that for sure," Kulik said. "Besides, until we come up with a better alternative, it is the only choice we have. Don't those American detective shows you've been watching say that the criminal always returns to the scene of the crime? Perhaps that is what the men who now have Pearce will do. At this bend in the road, Lensky, it is the only option we have."

Feeling defeated, Lensky sank into the sofa. "Very well. We will put a watch on the Pearce home. But surely we cannot run the risk of planting more dead KGB agents on the Pearce front lawn?"

"We cannot," Kulik said. "I was thinking of sending that American gangster you recruited when we first arrived. Do you still know how to contact him?"

"I have the telephone number where he can be reached," Lensky confirmed.

"Excellent." Major Kulik clapped his hands together. "Then I suggest you give him a call. We will want him watching the Pearce home as soon as possible. Oh, and given what happened last night to Blinov and the others, we cannot be too careful. It might be a good idea if this gangster of yours takes along a few of his friends."

"That should not pose a problem," Lensky said. "Of course, it will cost us more if he does."

"So we pay them," Kulik said. "As long as they do as they are hired to do, I don't care what they cost."

"And if something goes wrong, Major?"

"Like we say of our unfortunate cousins in Siberia, Lensky—better them than us."

6

As Calvin James, Karl Hahn and David McCarter pulled up to the main entrance of the Albert Risson Computer Camp, a thin man dressed in a pale-gray uniform stepped out of a guard shack to greet them.

"Evening," the man said. "Can I help you gentlemen?"

James smiled and leaned out the car window. "Yes, please. We're wondering if you could tell us where we could find Robert Pearce Jr.?"

"Sure," the man said. He walked into the guard shack and returned seconds later with a bright-yellow sticker and a photocopy of a map. "You tape the sticker inside the lower left corner of your windshield," he instructed, passing the sticker to James, who immediately followed the guard's orders.

"How's that?" James asked.

"Just fine, mister," the guard answered. "Now to find Bobby Pearce, you just go straight through the gate and then take a right at the first stop sign you come to. Bobby likes to get a few licks in at our computer lab. You'll find him on the second floor of the third building you hit after you make the turn. You can't miss it. But in case you do," he passed James the map, "this here'll help you."

"Thanks," James said, accepting the map.

The guard leaned forward. "That Bobby Pearce sure is popular."

"Is that so?"

"Yes, sir. You and your friends are the third carload in less than five minutes to be asking after the boy."

"Oh, shit!" James swore, pushing the accelerator to the floor and sending the Mercury Grand Marquis screeching through the main gate.

"Looks like we're catching the tail end of the party," McCarter offered, removing his 9 mm Browning autoloader from the Bianchi rig beneath his left arm. "The yobbos got here before we did."

James sent the Merc rocketing through the stop sign and squealed around the turn to the right. As soon as he had straightened out the car, he reached into his shoulder holster and withdrew a Colt Commander.

"Two carloads, the guard at the gate said." James flicked his eyes to the side as they passed the first of the buildings the guard had mentioned. "If there are four to six guys per car, we could be heading for a whole lotta heat."

Karl Hahn, riding in the back seat, took out his Walther P-5 automatic. "And if they've already got the boy, the miserable cowards probably won't be above using the youth as a shield."

The second building on the street flashed by.

"Yeah," James barked, "well, whatever the case, we can't let the bastards leave the computer camp with him. If we do that I'll bet we'll never see him *or* his father again. Hang on."

James gave the engine an extra boost of gas as they drew closer to building number three. He then braked and expertly slotted the Mercury into a space between two Ford Lincolns. Both the Fords were empty. McCarter and Hahn were already out of the car by the time James killed the engine.

"Cocky bunch," McCarter said, noting the Fords. "Didn't even feel the need to have somebody watch their cars."

"That's their trouble." James hopped from the Mercury and quickly covered the distance to the first of the Lincolns. His left hand flashed to the Jackass Leather rig under his right arm and removed a G-96 Boot 'n' Belt knife. Then he knelt and slashed one of the Ford's tires.

Air hissed from the rubbery wound while James ran to the other car to complete the job. He resheathed his knife and said to his partners, "Let's go."

The building that the Phoenix Force trio raced toward was two stories high. An air conditioner could be heard humming on top of its long flat roof. A brick walkway led to the double glass doors that opened into the building. Only half of the lights decorating the area in front of the structure were on because it was the weekend; the overall effect created pockets of shadows everywhere they looked.

Storming the building was senseless; it would be an open invitation to death. As anxious as the Stony Man warriors were to reach Bobby Pearce, their years spent surviving the murderous whims of combat had taught them many lessons, one of the most important being that graves were full of those too careless to take the time to do things right.

The Phoenix pros kept to the shadows as they silently advanced on the building. James traveled off to the left of the brick walkway, while Hahn and McCarter progressed to the right. Then they were at the building and moving toward the double glass doors, their weapons held in combat readiness. There was nothing to indicate their foes had actually posted a watch inside the doors, but the possibility existed.

Calvin James signaled that he would be the first to enter the building. Each of the doors opened outward, a definite obstacle if some trigger-happy clown was guarding the door from inside. James cautiously peered around the corner. From what he could see, the corridor beyond the doorway was clear. It was now or never. The black commando made his move.

With McCarter and Hahn ready to attack if James was challenged, the former Navy SEAL stepped away from the side of the building and onto the brick walkway. With his Colt Commander aimed in readiness, James gripped the handle of the door and pulled it open. A glance to his friends assured the Briton and West German that it was safe to enter. McCarter did so with Hahn following closely behind him.

The corridor was dimly lit and devoid of any unusual noises. Cool air conditioning flooded the hall. James shuddered, his alert senses telling him that the men they were seeking had passed this way. This was confirmed when James nudged open the first door in the hallway. Inside the tiny room, amid assorted buckets, mops and floor wax, was the body of a man in his mid to late fifties. The body was slumped on an overturned box of detergent, the head twisted at an awkward angle that left no doubt how the poor man had died. A jagged and bloody slash across the side of his head was proof enough that the janitor's sadistic killers had wanted to make sure he was dead.

Disgusted, James eased the maintenance room door shut, and he and his two companions moved on, going less than fifteen feet before they reached an elevator. The doors to the lift were closed and apparently could only be opened by staff members possessing a special access key. But taking the elevator was out of the question, in any case. Now knowing for certain that the killers were inside the building, the Phoenix Force teammates had to believe that the elevator was under surveillance on the second floor.

The hallway then branched into separate corridors leading to the left and right. A sign on the wall said that stairs could be found in both directions. James motioned that he would continue alone to the left, while McCarter and Hahn indicated they would stick with the corridor to the right. After determining it was safe to proceed, the three men hurried to their respective goals.

Calvin James had almost made it to the stairway when a burly Hispanic, with a full head of hair and a .38 revolver in his hand, unexpectedly appeared at the bottom of the steps. The shaggy gunman gasped in surprise, then spun on his feet as he aimed his weapon.

James dove through the air, slamming into his opponent with a forward tackle before the gunman could fire. Air whooshed from the Hispanic's lungs as the Phoenix commando and his would-be killer tumbled to the slick hallway floor.

When the pair hit the tiles, James's Colt went sailing. The gunman's .38 came swinging at the black tiger's head. James caught the descending wrist with both hands and viciously squeezed the flesh between his fingers. Carpethead grunted and shook like a fish on the end of a line. James continued to mangle the man's wrist and the .38 slipped from the Hispanic's grasp.

But the longhaired thug was just getting started. His free hand flashed into the pocket of his jeans and quickly produced a pearl-handled switchblade. Metal sang, but James rolled away before the tough's knife could find his flesh.

James stood, coming out of his massive maneuver with his own G-96 Boot 'n' Belt blade withdrawn in a reverse hold and ready for business. Schooled in the art of knife fighting when a youth in Chicago, James confidently faced his attacker.

The Hispanic leaped to his feet and charged, the knife in his hand stabbing toward the Phoenix pro's midsection. James sidestepped to his opponent's left rear, at the same time blocking, trapping and redirecting the thrusting switchblade. The G-96 caught the outmatched hood with an inverted slash across the stomach.

"¡Carajo!" grunted the object of James's attention.

James whirled in a half circle as he thrust his own knife into his opponent. Longhair gurgled in despair. Locking his grip with the man's hand that still held the switchblade, James swung out his leg and swept his foe off his feet. The twice-wounded killer fell to the floor.

James followed him in a blur of fluid motion, dropping to a kneeling position while simultaneously pulling his enemy's arm back and down upon his upraised knee. The Hispanic's arm broke with a sharp snap and his switchblade dropped the few inches to the floor. James completed his attack by forcing the G-96 deep into the doomed killer's throat. The man's body jerked beneath the attack. James twisted his knife and pulled the blade free. The man was dead.

"And that's the way it's done," James said softly, wiping his blade clean and resheathing the weapon. He recovered his Colt and glanced behind to the opposite end of the corridor. McCarter and Hahn were gone, already on their way to the second floor. James crossed to the nearby stairwell and started up the steps.

ASSURED THAT CALVIN JAMES would effectively dispatch his lone adversary, McCarter and Hahn hurriedly rushed upstairs. Speed and timing were crucial now. The man James was fighting had probably been sent downstairs to check on the security status of the first floor. Would someone come looking for him if he failed to report back? Or what if James's rival began screaming for help? Such loud noises in the quiet building would surely be noticed.

They heard voices before reaching the second-floor landing—two or more males conversing in hushed Spanish tones. McCarter took the lead and cautiously peered around the corner. Halfway down the hall, four armed men were exiting from what McCarter assumed was the computer lab. The four had their backs to the Englishman and were focusing their concentration on someone still inside the room. There was no sign of young Bobby Pearce.

McCarter pulled back from the landing and held up four fingers to Hahn. The BND-trained warrior nodded, then signaled his readiness to proceed. McCarter looked around the corner again and observed that the four gunmen had stepped farther into the hallway; their backs were still turned to the two Phoenix commandos.

Gripping his Browning Hi-Power, McCarter silently began advancing down the corridor. Hahn followed the Cockney's example moments later.

As McCarter and Hahn gingerly made their approach along the dimly lit hallway, one of the gunmen broke away from the group, and headed toward the stairwell at the far end of the corridor. He had almost reached his destination when he turned to say something to his friends. Instantly, he spotted McCarter and Hahn and then all hell broke loose.

"¡Joder!" the gunman exclaimed.

The Briton, unsure of where Bobby Pearce was and unwilling to risk the boy's life in a dangerous firefight, shouted, *"¡No se mueva!"*

The Phoenix commando's order that nobody move was totally ignored. The first to disobey the command was the hoodlum who had sounded the alarm. Wielding an Astra Model 357, the crud with the twenty-twenty vision tried to bag McCarter with a poorly aimed shot from the hip that never took off. McCarter's autoloader cracked twice, the combined doses of 9 mm thunder effectively putting the sharp-eyed criminal's career on permanent hold. One Browning bullet chewed through the gunman's shoulder; the follow-up shot did the same to the killer's heart. The man collapsed in a miserable bundle of death.

The remaining three men in the hallway reacted to their friend's shouted warning with varying degrees of speed. One thug, faster on the uptake than his pals, tried to blast McCarter where he stood with the aid of a Detonics Mk VI. Hahn anticipated the gunman's intentions and brought them to a swift, irrevocable end, courtesy of his own Walther P-5. Three times Hahn's gun barked. The first P-5 missile missed. The final two did not.

The death carriers slammed into his face with a one-two punch from which he would never recover. The man in Hahn's sights died showering his friends with a sticky spray of blood, brains and bone chips. The shower was going full blast as the lifeless body fell to the floor.

If the remaining two gunmen were reconsidering their recent decision to go against McCarter's order, they did a nice job of concealing the fact by unleashing a burning salvo of lead down the hallway at McCarter and Hahn. Both Phoenix Force soldiers leaped for cover, each of the Stony Man favorites seeking refuge in the recessed doorways of nearby rooms. Enemy bullets chased the pair every inch of the way, transforming the walls of the corridor into an impromptu design of slug-punctured plaster.

The shooting stopped and McCarter glimpsed around the doorway, immediately pulling back after a fresh enemy bullet gouged a hole in the wall above his head. From what he could tell, the two gunmen had tucked themselves away in similar recessed areas farther along the hall.

McCarter's position was diagonally across from the computer lab. The doorway Hahn stood in was also on the same side of the corridor. As the Briton watched, Hahn turned and tested the door behind him. It was unlocked. Nodding farewell to McCarter, Hahn opened the door and disappeared inside.

The room Hahn entered was an audiovisual classroom. Moonlight streamed through an open window, providing just enough light to see by. A video tape recorder and wide-screen television were set up at one end, with a raked audience section arranged directly opposite. A narrow aisle running between the seats ended at a doorway on the far wall. Hahn made his way toward this door.

Outside in the corridor, more gunshots were fired, but whether they came from McCarter or their trigger-happy opponents, Hahn could not tell. He reached the door at the rear of the room and gently tested its handle, discovering that this door was also unlocked. Going through it would take him into the room next door and, he hoped, into the computer lab. As the hot and heavy battle in the hallway continued, Hahn slowly turned the handle with his left hand and eased the door open.

The door was torn from his grip as an invisible fist collided with the side of the West German's head. A vista of shooting stars exploded behind his eyes. Something hard thudded against Hahn's wrist. His Walther P-5 took flight. Then a powerful pair of hands grabbed hold of Hahn's clothes and forcibly yanked the Phoenix warrior off his feet and through the doorway.

Hahn was in the computer lab. He digested that fact just before he plowed into a table that sent one IBM system and its hard disk drive spilling with a crash to the floor. A sound came from behind him, and Hahn rolled quickly to the right, pushing away from the knocked-over table as a long, wooden broomstick struck the exact location where his head had been. Unprepared for such an unyielding target as the overturned table, the broomstick snapped in two.

Karl Hahn jumped to his feet and turned to confront his assailant—a squatly-built Hispanic with a pencil-thin mustache. The sharp, broken end of the broomstick was in the Hispanic's hand, slashing back and forth like a large, ugly splinter. More gunshots came from the hallway, and someone screamed in mortal agony.

Doubt momentarily registered on the Hispanic's face at the sound of the scream, and then he was charging forward, whipping the pointed stick he carried from side to side. Hahn retreated to avoid the jagged weapon, but he was limited to taking three steps in reverse before he bumped into another table, this one holding a computer with two disk drives.

Convinced Hahn was trapped and finished, the confident Hispanic advanced with his evil toothpick. Hahn turned unexpectedly, his right hand sweeping over the surface of the table in search of something to defend himself with. A practitioner in the art of improvised weaponry, Hahn's fingers quickly closed upon something.

The object in Hahn's hand was a 5.25-inch floppy disk, and as he danced to the left to avoid his enemy's attack, Hahn inserted his index finger into the diskette's spindle hole, while deftly curling his thumb around the floppy's outer edge.

"Kommen Sie hier, Schwanzgesicht!" Hahn taunted his rival.

The Hispanic blinked at the sight of the floppy disk Hahn held and then he laughed. The madman who did not even speak English was trying to threaten him with a tiny piece of plastic. *¡Muy loco!* The foreign fool would be an easy kill, impaled on the end of the broken broomstick like a slow-moving marsh frog.

The Hispanic swung the broomstick in a downward blow aimed at Hahn's chest. Before it connected, Hahn stepped aside and lashed out with a rapid slice of the floppy disk in his hand. Plastic met flesh and the Hispanic let out a high-pitched yell.

Hahn's attacker glanced at the injury and blanched when he saw a bright ribbon of blood appear along his forearm. A fifteen-stitch wound if ever he saw one!

"Now you die!" the furious Hispanic promised, ignoring his bleeding arm as he renewed his attack—not blindly clutching his stick weapon as he had previously done, but now clutching one end of the stick in each hand as he lowered his head and charged.

Like a matador in a losing contest with an enraged bull, Hahn was hit and half-carried, half-thrown against the nearest wall. The broken broomstick struck him flat across the chest, and his lungs emptied of air. Then the broomstick that was pressing his body began sliding upward—straight for his throat.

Hahn fought with one hand to prevent the Hispanic's weapon from choking him to death, while he used his other hand to saw the floppy disk back and forth over his adversary's neck and shoulders. Hahn knew the plastic disk was doing some sort of damage because he could feel a wash of warm blood splashing over his hands. But even this failed to discourage the determined Hispanic from trying to force the broken broomstick over Hahn's chest and down on the West German's throat.

Hahn's life was being squeezed out of him as his left hand shaped itself into a claw and dug into the hair at the back of the Hispanic's head. The Phoenix Force warrior flexed the muscles of his arm, pulling his enemy's head upright. Blood was splattered over the Hispanic's face, but the man was grinning, smiling at Hahn because the West German was about to die.

The floppy disk he held was bent and battered as Hahn managed to sweep one edge of the disk across the bridge of the Hispanic's nose. Fresh blood spurted from the cut, and Hahn turned his hand so that a corner of the disk dug into his opponent's eye. The delicate orb succumbed to the assault and ruptured with a burst of corneal tissue. An unholy moan of anguish broke from the blinded Hispanic's lips.

Stumbling away from Hahn in a shrieking fit, the man threw the broomstick to the floor and, clamping his hands over his ruined eye, ran headlong into the barrier of a closed window. Glass shattered from the impact, and the screaming Hispanic lost his balance and fell through the razor-sharp hole. He took the ride of his life to the ground below.

Hahn massaged some of the pain from his throat as he searched for and found his Walther P-5. A final muffled gunshot came from the corridor, and then Hahn heard McCarter's voice through the doorway.

"Karl?" McCarter called. "Are you okay, mate?"

"Fine," Hahn returned, his voice raspy. He located a light switch and was about to turn it on when

McCarter and James entered the lab. "What about the gunmen?"

"I nailed one," the British commando said. "Calvin captured the other."

"Where is he?" Hahn asked.

"Sleeping off a headache on the steps leading down to the first floor," James said. "I clobbered him one with my Colt. We'll pick him up on the way out."

Hahn switched on the lights.

"Damn!" James swore.

Slumped in the far corner of the room beside the computer where he had been working was Bobby Pearce. The boy was stretched out on the floor with a discarded hypodermic syringe next to his thigh. The three men crossed to the youth, and James knelt to check the kid's pulse.

"Weak, but it's there," James offered, hefting the weight of the unconscious boy onto his shoulders. "He's out cold."

McCarter kicked at the hypodermic. "Right miserable bastards. How much courage does it take for a pack of scum to square off with one kid?"

"Let's talk about it in the car," James suggested. "The boy ain't my brother, but he's heavy."

7

"This gig sucks, man," Rupert Horner protested. "The mosquitoes are eating me alive."

"How much longer do we have to wait?" Jackie Reeves wanted to know.

"Yeah," Tommy Stiles added, "my feet are killing me."

"Shut up, all of you," snapped Rick Marcella. "We'll damn well wait until I say it's time to stop waiting. Understand? I don't know why you're bitchin'. So far, you're getting paid a couple of bills each just to take a ride in the country with me. Plus you get to enjoy the warm night air. What's so bad about that?"

"We've been doing it for more than two whole hours," Horner said. "Watching that house over there and feeding the local insect population. How're we ever gonna collect any bonus money if nobody shows up for us to capture? Huh? How about explaining that?"

Marcella regarded the whining Horner and resisted the urge to brass knuckle the younger man's nose into pulp. Horner was a first-class griper, and if the need to recruit some extra muscle had not popped up on such short notice, Marcella told himself he would have left Horner and the other pair of losers back in L.A.

Next time, Marcella decided, he would insist on more than an hour or two to package a job. No matter how long it took to bring the right combination of manpower together, it would be worth the effort. Anything was better than getting saddled with losers. Marcella hated many things in life, but most of all he hated working with amateurs.

Rick Marcella's education in crime had begun at the tender age of ten when he started a protection racket at school. For a payment of fifty cents a week, his fellow classmates were guaranteed that no one, especially not Ricky Marcella, would be waiting to beat the stuffing out of them after school.

As the years passed, his nickel-and-dime schemes took a back seat to bolder ventures. Marcella was eager and willing to dabble in all the activities frowned upon by law-abiding citizens: shoplifting, home burglary and auto theft.

At sixteen, he was ready for some heavier action, and he participated in his first armed robbery. A liquor store clerk was wounded during the holdup, and Marcella was later arrested and identified by the clerk. Brought before a judge, Marcella lowered his head in shame and pleaded guilty, telling the judge that he had fallen in with the wrong crowd and vowing to walk the straight and narrow.

The sympathetic magistrate bought the story that the accused had seen the error of his ways, and Marcella was given a one-year suspended sentence. If Marcella learned anything from the experience it was that, no matter what the job, the only way to get away clean was to never leave a witness.

Drafted and subsequently discharged as unfit for service, Marcella's status as a crook who knew the ropes grew with each successful job he pulled. More often than not he worked alone, but when a special heist required accomplices, the enterprising criminal always handpicked his team. This was especially true on breaking and entering exercises. Marcella's share from a single, well-planned haul was frequently enough to grease his gears for months at a time.

When he was twenty-one, a jewelry store robbery went sour with the clanging of a burglar alarm. The smug owner of the store actually had the nerve to laugh at the would-be thief when the alarm began to ring. Marcella erased the store owner's smile with a point-blank shot to the center of the forehead. He then made his escape before the police could arrive.

The failed robbery attempt was the turning point in Rick Marcella's career. When the realization came that he had committed a murder and not been caught, his business sense told him that such a skill could really bring in the bucks. His intuition was correct, and in the ensuing years, he performed no less than seventeen contract killings.

Lately, business had been slow and Marcella had taken to spending his time putting away tall, cool ones in a bar near his apartment. This is what he had been doing two weeks before when a man he had never met struck up a conversation.

The man spoke with a foreign accent and said his name was Leonard. Marcella could not have cared less. What did pique his interest was the way Leo wasted no time at all getting down to the nitty-gritty. Leonard, it seemed, was looking to lay down some cash as a retainer against an unnamed job in the future. As Leo saw it, a guy who was not overly sensitive about what he had to do to fatten his bank balance could benefit nicely from such an arrangement.

Marcella saw it the same way. He had accepted a down payment for undisclosed services and then had given Leo a phone number where he could be reached. Leo had contacted him earlier in the evening.

Leo wanted Marcella to watch a private home out in Piru, a small town fifty miles north of Los Angeles. If anyone showed up nosing around the place, Marcella was to encourage them to go for a ride that would eventually lead them to Leonard. Marcella's advance for the stakeout was one thousand dollars, with a bonus five times that amount if he delivered someone to Leonard.

Merely as a precaution, Marcella was advised to take along three or four of his friends, each of whom he was authorized to pay five hundred dollars. Marcella accepted the assignment and then met briefly with Leonard, who handed over the twenty-five hundred dollars—a thousand for him and the remaining fifteen for Marcella's three accomplices.

Marcella paid the three men two hundred dollars each and kept the rest for himself. Leonard may have been willing to fork out five hundred each for the likes of Horner, Reeves and Stiles, but Marcella was not.

And so, Marcella thought as he slapped at a mosquito that had landed on his arm, here they were. Four armed men staring at an empty house and waiting.

Until someone showed up, there was nothing else to do. Just bide their time and watch the house.

And wait.

8

Yakov Katzenelenbogen and Gary Manning let themselves into Robert Pearce's house with a key provided by Hal Brognola. Manning located a light switch near the front door and flipped it up, turning on a small table lamp nearby. Katz locked the door behind them.

"First things first," the Israeli colonel said.

They went to the kitchen where Katz checked the back door. It was locked with a dead bolt and chained. Reassuring, but not good enough for Katz. Going to the cupboards, both he and Manning rummaged through them until the Canadian's arms were full of metal pots and pans.

"Are we expecting guests for dinner?" Manning asked.

Katz shook his head. "But one never knows, does one?"

With Manning watching, Katz took half of the utensils held by his Canadian counterpart and tied them against the back door. The two men returned to the front door and repeated the procedure.

"There," the Israeli said. "It's a rather crude alarm system, but it'll do. Most of our investigation will be upstairs." He pointed to the tiny tower of skillets and saucepans that he had constructed. "This way if company calls, we're going to know about it. Shall we?''

Together they climbed the carpeted steps to the second floor and began combing the rooms for clues. From one side of the house to the other they searched, opening drawers, looking through closets, concentrating their efforts on trying to find anything that would help identify Robert Pearce's captors.

They drew a blank with the master bedroom. Nothing was out of place. The same was true of Bobby Pearce's room. It was actually cleaner and neater than his father's.

''This sure doesn't look like the room I had when I was a teenager,'' Manning remarked.

Instead of walls decorated with the garish faces of rock stars who were still waiting patiently for their first whisker or of athletes whose sportsmanship was measured by the size of their latest contract, the only celebrity posted in Bobby Pearce's room was Albert Einstein, staring out from a miniature picture frame set on top of a dresser.

By the time they reached the room that served as an office for Pearce and his son, Katz and Manning were thoroughly disappointed. With no solid leads to the identity of Robert Pearce's abductors, their chances of isolating a positive clue that evening were depressingly slim.

''I hope to hell the others have had more luck than us,'' a frustrated Manning said as they entered the final room of their second-floor search. ''Unless we've made a glaring oversight, the people who have Pearce didn't leave anything behind.''

''It sure doesn't look like it, Gary.''

Katz crossed to the desk in the far corner of the room. A computer system occupied much of the space on the desk. An amber light glowing at the edge of the system's right disk drive told them that the computer was on. Katz held out his left index finger and randomly pressed one of the keys on the computer's console. Instantly, the system's CRT video display flashed to life, and line after line of complex formulas appeared on the monitor's screen.

"See." Manning pointed. "The last line of the program is much shorter than the rest."

"Which probably means that Robert Pearce was working at the computer when the three KGB operatives made their move to grab him." Katz leaned down for a closer examination of the screen. "Hal was right. If this program is an example of Robert Pearce's expertise, the work his son is capable of must be awesome. What do you think?"

Manning's reply was interrupted by the sound of pots and pans crashing to the floor. Katz and the Canadian made eye contact, a silent understanding passing between them. No words were necessary. Katz's makeshift alarm system had paid off; the seasoned Stony Man veterans would take it from there.

Katzenelenbogen was armed with the Uzi submachine gun that he usually depended upon in combat. As a backup piece, he carried a SIG-Sauer P-226 9 mm pistol. Manning's weapons included a Desert Eagle .357 worn in a shoulder rig and a .41 Magnum S&W revolver with an eight-inch barrel in a cross-draw holster on his belt.

With his .357 in hand, Manning quietly left the Pearces' home office and started down the hallway toward the stairs. Katz, his Uzi held in his left hand and supported by his hooked prosthesis, followed closely behind. As they approached the staircase, the sounds of disgusted male voices could be heard from below.

"What the hell are you trying to do?" one voice hissed. "Wake up the whole damn—"

"I didn't know the pans were there!" a second voice protested.

"Amateurs!" the first voice complained. "Get going! And make sure you don't kill both of 'em. We don't get a bonus without a prisoner."

Footsteps beat across the floor as one or more of the invaders headed toward the stairs. Manning waited until the strangers were halfway to the second floor before welcoming the uninvited guests. Swinging his .357 around the corner of the hallway, Manning opened fire, catching a pair of gun-toting fools off guard.

Four times Gary Manning worked the semiauto's trigger, sending two bursts of death to each of his targets. The gunmen were impossible to miss.

Gunman number one permanently retired when the pair of 158-grain bullets stormed through his body in all the wrong places. The first bullet disintegrated ribs and transformed his left lung into lumpy red jelly, while the follow-up shot totally destroyed the grillwork of five capped teeth. The back of the intruder's head took a powder as the bullet kept traveling.

Manning's second target caught both of the Eagle's .357 eggs in the breadbasket. Blood gushed from the dual wounds as the man's stomach, liver and gallbladder became indistinguishable. The dying man dropped the .38 six-shooter he was carrying and doubled over screaming. He lost his balance and fell backward down the stairs.

Manning pulled back out of sight just as a double-barreled shotgun thundered from the base of the steps, the brunt of the terrible blasts chewing ham-sized holes in the corner of the wall beside the Canadian's head. The noise was still ringing in the air when the two Phoenix commandos heard the front door slam.

"Damn!" swore Manning. "They're getting away!"

"That's what they think," Katz corrected.

Aware that it could easily be a ploy to lure them into the open, Katz and Manning were forced to cautiously descend the stairs, their senses keyed to the possibility of an ambush. No such attack materialized. By the time they reached the bottom of the steps, it became clear that the remaining killers had fled the Pearce home.

"Think they're waiting to nail us outside?" Manning asked.

"It's possible," Katz admitted. "If I were them, I'd try to pick us off as we stepped through the doorway. Of course, they could just as easily have kept going. There's only one sure way of finding out."

"I know," Manning said. "Where's McCarter when we really need him?"

They approached the open doorway from the left side, taking care to keep themselves hidden from view. The table lamp they had switched on when they had first entered the house was now off; a stroke of good fortune for the Phoenix duo. The last thing they wanted when they were ready to make their move through the doorway was to be backlit.

Once in the living room, Katz crossed to the picture window that faced onto the front yard. Pulling aside the edge of the curtain, he looked outside. Satisfied, he lowered the curtain into place.

"Well?" Manning whispered.

"Nothing but the car we drove up in," Katz replied in hushed tones. "No sign of anybody."

"The bastards are out there. I can feel it."

"They could be hiding behind our rental."

"That's what I was thinking," Manning said. He moved closer to the doorway and motioned for Katzenelenbogen to follow. "Let's see if I can't flush them out. Cover me."

The Israeli cradled his Uzi. "You got it."

Manning nodded. "Here I go."

Gripping his .357 tightly in his fist, Manning charged through the open doorway, turned to his right and dove for the hedge. As soon as the Canadian had appeared in the doorway, two enemy gunmen popped up from behind the Hertz rental. The killer nearest Manning wielded a double-barreled shotgun while his partner carried a Colt A-2 Sporter II semiautomatic rifle.

"No!" Katz shouted as he leaped into the doorway. Before the distracted gunmen could decide exactly who they should shoot first, the decision was permanently taken out of their hands.

Working the business end of his SMG in a back and forth motion, Katz hosed down the gunmen with a deadly downpour of 9 mm raindrops. Dancing in unison to the Uzi's compelling, heavy metal music, the killers twitched and jerked in the throes of death. The shotgun discharged and the windshield of the Hertz rental shattered. Then the owner of the double-barrel collapsed to the driveway in a heap of dying agony.

The hood sporting the Sporter II assault rifle waltzed to his grave with his body leaking blood from a dozen different holes. By the time the Uzi's twenty-five round magazine ran dry, the killer was already history.

Katz stepped from the doorway, and Manning picked himself up off the ground.

"You okay?" Katz asked.

"Fine, thanks. How'd we do?"

"Four up, four down," Katz said.

"But without any prisoners, we're back to square one."

"It's not like they gave us a choice."

"Yeah," Manning said. "Next time they'll know better." He went to the bodies sprawled on the driveway and then examined the front seat of the car. It was covered with broken glass. The Canadian turned and looked at his Israeli friend. "Katz, when it comes time to return this car to the rental agency, I'm going to let *you* do the talking."

9

Armando Torres-Quinteros had a problem.

He was the *jefe*, or chief, of one of Mexico's twelve most prominent criminal families. Together the twelve organizations formed what the U.S. Drug Enforcement Administration referred to as the Mexican Mafia.

For years, the Torres-Quinteros clan had limited itself to the activities usually associated with society's underbelly. Their endeavors ran the gamut from gunrunning and smuggling to narcotics. Business was good and a fiscal year rarely passed without the clan substantially increasing their already burgeoning coffers.

When he inherited control of the clan, Armando Torres-Quinteros vowed he would do everything within his power to see that the family interests thrived as never before. The enterprising Mexican lived up to his promise, which explained why his family was one of the first to join MERGE, an international alliance of evil.

MERGE's ranks consisted of four previously divergent criminal groups. Topping the list was the infamous Union d'Corse, or the Corsican Syndicate. The

Union d'Corse controlled MERGE operations based in and around Western Europe.

The powerful Colombian Syndicate was also a paying member in the alliance. Headquartered in Central America, the Colombian branch of MERGE devoted itself to the lucrative cocaine trade so prevalent in Florida and on the rest of the east coast of the United States.

Black syndicates responsible for the rampant crime rate that dominated ghetto neighborhoods throughout the U.S. were also connected to MERGE. When the call to duty was sounded, the largest and most organized of the black syndicates were among the first to enlist.

The Mexican Mafia quickly followed suit. Armando Torres-Quinteros and his cohorts in the "Mexican Connection" had always profited from their business transactions, but they were constantly on the lookout for new worlds to conquer. MERGE was a step in the right direction and its directors lost no time in providing their Mexican partners with fresh, cash-producing schemes.

In the beginning, everyone connected with MERGE made money. The gravy train was rolling down the tracks of success, and it was easy to think that the ride would never end. Then came the cold, sobering defeat of a MERGE operation in the Bahamas, immediately followed by another in San Francisco.

Stung by the collapse of two carefully orchestrated plans, as well as the deaths of numerous MERGE soldiers, MERGE retreated to the shadows to lick its wounds and count its losses.

And that brought Armando Torres-Quinteros back to his problem. In forty-two years, he had never learned to be patient, especially when he was convinced there was some easy money to be made. When he could sit by the sidelines no longer, he decided that the Torres-Quinteros family would try something new—in this instance, some good, old-fashioned kidnapping.

Armando Torres-Quinteros never did anything by half measures. Once he had made up his mind, he naturally set his sights on someone who would bring in the most amount of money for the least amount of effort and risk. After narrowing his list of likely candidates to five individuals, including one U.S. senator and an American television talk show host, the Mexican decided that the logical bird to shoot for was Robert Pearce.

This choice was no accident. Having read a biographical profile on Pearce in a weekly newsmagazine, Torres-Quinteros had no doubt that Pearce was the man he was looking for. According to the article, Robert Pearce was one of the United States's foremost computer programmers. In that capacity, Pearce freely admitted to the interviewer that he was involved in certain "high-level" government projects that he was not at liberty to discuss. Such an admission could only mean one thing: Robert Pearce's undisclosed government projects had to be tied in with the U.S. Department of Defense.

Although it was not originally a venture sanctioned by MERGE, Torres-Quinteros had little difficulty convincing the criminal cartel that kidnapping Robert Pearce would be an effective way to raise some easy *dinero*. Only one day after formally presenting his plan to MERGE, the Mexican was given approval to follow through with his scheme.

Within forty-eight hours Robert Pearce was taken, but only after the men sent to kidnap him had disposed of three armed gunmen also intent on abducting Pearce. If the Mexicans had arrived ten minutes later, they would have come away from Pearce's home empty-handed.

And the identities of the three gunmen? So far, the evidence suggested that the trio were Soviet agents working in the United States. Armando Torres-Quinteros had digested that unexpected piece of information with pleasure. Now, instead of just one party interested in acquiring Pearce, he had two. Wonderful. It was the same kind of business atmosphere he appreciated when dealing with narcotics. Nothing compared to the excitement, or profit, of conducting a sale in a seller's market.

The Mexican's idea to kidnap Robert Pearce's son also was really an afterthought. Pearce was much more likely to cooperate if he knew his captors had taken his son prisoner, too.

But now, at least two hours after his men should have returned with Bobby Pearce as their prize, Armando Torres-Quinteros was regretting his decision to kidnap the boy. His gut instinct told him that something had happened to his men. His sixth sense warned him that possibly all of his soldiers were dead.

That any of his men would betray the operation was unthinkable. The code of conduct adhered to within the families of the Mexican Mafia was known as *cosa de hombre*, a man's thing. It dictated that any kind of betrayal, lying or cheating within the family be punishable by death. There were no exceptions to the rule.

Armando Torres-Quinteros did not believe that any of his men would willingly do anything disloyal. But, as *jefe* of his clan, it was his duty to protect his people. If there was the slightest possibility that someone outside of the family knew where Robert Pearce was being held, then it was his responsibility to render that knowledge useless.

He reached across his desk and pushed a button on his intercom. Within seconds, his sister's eldest son entered the room.

"Yes, Uncle?" The young man was properly respectful. "You wish something?"

Torres-Quinteros nodded. "I am concerned that Elias and the others have not yet returned with Pearce's son. It is my belief that they have run into trouble. If so, we cannot take the chance of that trouble finding us. Alert our people that we move out at once."

"As you wish, Uncle. And Robert Pearce?"

Torres-Quinteros opened a drawer in his desk and withdrew a zippered pouch that he then slid across to his nephew.

"See that our guest is prepared to travel," he said.

The young man took the leather pouch. "As you wish, Uncle."

MAJOR VIKTOR KULIK SAT wringing his hands, his eyes dancing from the clock on the wall to the front door and then back to the clock again. It was four-fifteen in the morning, and Captain Oleg Lensky still had not returned.

Kulik managed to sip his warm flat beer. He stared at the silent telephone resting beside him on the sofa. At the very least, Lensky could have called if there was a problem. Was that asking too much? Kulik snarled at the phone. Apparently, it was.

The major rubbed his tired eyes. He should have been in bed and sleeping. Where the hell was Lensky?

"Wha—"

A key turning in the lock woke Kulik up. He had dozed off. He squinted at the clock. Four-forty-eight. Almost five. He blinked.

Then the door opened and Lensky entered. Kulik demanded an explanation before the door was closed.

"And just where have you been?"

Lensky crossed to the living room and flopped into an armchair. "Do we have any more beer? I'm thirsty."

"You can drink later, Comrade. Answer my question."

"Where do you think I've been? I've been waiting since midnight to hear from that gangster you insisted we use."

"Are you speaking of the criminal *you* recruited for the job, Lensky? Rick Marcella, I believe his name was."

"Let's get something straight. I sent Marcella and three of his friends to spy on the Pearce home because I was ordered to. You said that I must learn to follow orders, and that is what I was doing. You are the divisional control officer in Los Angeles, Major. Not me. How could I have possibly hired Marcella without your approval? Pull anything funny and our superiors in the Collegium are sure to ask some very embarrassing questions."

"And when they ask me, I shall tell them that you acted without my authorization," Kulik insisted. "You will be brought before the Collegium for insubordination."

"And you, Major, will be standing next to me to answer charges of losing control of the men under your command. Bah, how I hate injustice!"

Kulik knew when he was cornered. "Very well, Lensky. We will set aside our differences for now. Tell me about Marcella."

"There is nothing to tell," Lensky said. "All night long, I sat at this wretched drinking establishment waiting to hear from him. Marcella never phoned."

"Neither did you. The phone did not ring once."

"There was no point in calling," Lensky defended his actions. "The place I was in was so noisy you could not hear the television."

"I might have known that you were watching your precious American television programs. Remember, Lensky, every single word of your confession is going into my report."

"What confession?" Lensky moaned. "I have done nothing but follow your orders. You'll see, the Collegium will listen to my side of the story. I know they will."

"Undoubtedly," Kulik snapped almost gleefully. "Just before you are presented with a one-way ticket to Siberia."

"Over my dead body," Lensky challenged.

"That may be what our superiors will have in mind," Kulik agreed.

Lensky leaped from the armchair. "Listen, like it or not, Major, we are in this mess together. If the bears of the Collegium decide to get nasty, it will not matter whether it was you or I who hired those men to spy on the home of Robert Pearce.

"You know that they are never satisfied with negative results. Never. And don't forget about Blinov, Kaplenko and Solotrin. We still have to answer for them. And unless we deliver Robert Pearce, the Collegium is not going to like the answers they hear."

"So what do you suggest we do? I don't know about you, Captain, but I don't know how to pull a rabbit from a hat."

"Nor I," Lensky said. "But unless we do something to remedy the situation, I'm afraid that trick won't even help us."

"I go on record here and now," Kulik said, "that I do not particularly agree with your line of thinking. Nevertheless, you may be right. Am I to assume that the gangster and his friends are dead?"

"Draw your own conclusions. Marcella was to check in with me by two this morning. I never received his call. In answer to your question, then...yes, I believe we can assume that Marcella and his colleagues have joined Blinov and the others in that big Intourist Office in the sky."

"I see," Major Kulik said. "If that's the case, then obviously the people who kidnapped Robert Pearce are more dangerous than we expected. Are you a man inclined to prayer, Lensky?"

"You know I am not."

"Then perhaps it's time you started. We are running out of options, and unless one presents itself to us in the near future, then the Collegium is going to be playing kickball with our *mudak*," Kulik stood and stretched. "I'm going to bed. At this point, Lensky, can you think of anything constructive to say?"

"Yes," answered the captain, heading toward the kitchen. "I still want my beer."

10

The hit was a bust.

"No King Edward on this one, mates," McCarter said.

"From the looks of this place, we couldn't have missed them by more than an hour," James complained. "It's my fault. I shouldn't have waited so long to use the scopolamine on our prisoner."

"Don't blame yourself," Hahn advised. "For all we know, everyone was preparing to evacuate the premises anyway."

"Karl's right," Katz acknowledged. "They were probably planning to relocate to a new hideout all along. Even if we did spook them into flying the coop, at least now we have good reason to believe that Robert Pearce is still being held somewhere within the Los Angeles basin."

Having regrouped at their L.A. hotel, the Phoenix Force commandos deposited Bobby Pearce safely in bed and then went to work interrogating the man James had clobbered during the fight at the Albert Risson Computer Camp.

Upon awakening with one massive headache, the prisoner exhibited no indications of fear and proudly informed his captors that he would tell them nothing, not even his name.

"Beat me, torture me, do whatever you want," the Hispanic challenged them in a fit of indignation that turned his copper-colored complexion red with anger. "I am stronger than all of you put together. I will not talk."

"We know that, numb-nuts," James said. "And that is why we're going to have to find an easier method to make you sing."

"You're wasting your time," sneered the man. "I'm not afraid to die. You may as well shoot me now."

James nodded. "Exactly what I had in mind."

"What?" The incredulous prisoner strained against the ropes binding him to the straight-backed chair. "You would shoot an unarmed man?"

"Better living through chemistry," James replied, the former Navy medic producing a hypodermic syringe filled with scopolamine. "Say good-night."

And before the macho Mexican could say anything to pollute the air, Calvin James had injected the truth serum into the unwilling recipient. Finally, when the interrogation was finished, the Stony Man crew knew the name of their enemy.

"Son of a bitch!" James exclaimed as he and his Phoenix Force partners left their prisoner bound to his chair and retired to another room of their hotel suite. "MERGE again!"

"Don't those bastards know when to quit?" Manning wondered.

"MERGE," Hahn said, repeating the identity of Phoenix Force's common enemy as he turned to Katz.

"Aren't they the international crime organization you've mentioned?"

"MERGE is one of them," the Israeli commander confirmed. "The other is a vicious triumvirate out of the Orient called TRIO. Both organizations are deadly in their own right."

James explained, "MERGE took shape after factions of the Corsican Syndicate joined forces with the Colombian Syndicate, black syndicates here in the States and with the Mexican Mafia south of the border."

"Who evidently are the pack of rats behind nabbing Robert Pearce," McCarter said, sipping from an ice-cold can of Coke and grateful, not for the first time, that the soft drink firm had seen the light of day as far as the flavor of his favorite beverage was concerned. "From what I hear, the Mexican Mafia put some of their Italian namesakes to shame."

"I can think of three dead KGB agents who would agree with you," Manning commented, then he looked at James. "How far away is the building our prisoner said MERGE is using for its base of ops?"

"Not far," James answered. "Twenty miles tops. Taking the freeways should put us there in no time flat."

Leaving Gary Manning at the hotel to guard the sleeping Bobby Pearce, as well as to turn over their prisoner to the federal officers that Hal Brognola was sending over, the remaining Phoenix Force members gathered up their gear and left for the headquarters of MERGE. But even before entering the site, it became clear to the world's finest counterterrorists that they had arrived too late.

"There's nothing I hate more than getting to a party after everybody's left," McCarter said as he made his way from the cell Robert Pearce had been held in.

"Not much we can do about it now," Katz observed, "except head back to the hotel and try to develop a lead in some other direction."

"Now that we know MERGE definitely has Pearce," James said, "what happened at the Albert Risson Computer Camp makes more sense."

"Exactly," Hahn agreed. "Kidnapping Bobby Pearce would have given MERGE a matched set, father and son. I'm betting they really aren't aware of how Bobby fits into the scheme of things, though. They probably just wanted to abduct the boy to insure his father's cooperation."

"That's understandable," Katz said. "And since they didn't grab the boy, there's no telling what MERGE has in store for his dad. The thing that disturbs me is that MERGE has had Robert Pearce since Friday evening. That's two nights ago. It doesn't look like they're out to kill him, but if they did snatch Pearce as part of a daring kidnapping plot, then why hasn't MERGE contacted the authorities to issue their demands for his safe return?"

"Right," McCarter said. "It's to MERGE's advantage to do whatever they've got planned for Pearce and be done with it. The longer they hang on to him, the greater a liability he becomes. And after losing so many people in the attempt to kidnap Bobby Pearce, you have to believe MERGE won't want to hang onto Pearce any longer than it has to."

"And don't forget the Soviets," reminded Hahn. "They fit into this mess somehow. We know for sure they've already lost three of their operatives, and we all know what sore losers they are."

"Which means," James said, "that somewhere in Los Angeles, the KGB is probably looking for Pearce, too."

"Yeah," McCarter summed up the situation. "Let's hope we find him first."

11

"Where am I?"

Bobby Pearce opened his eyes and studied the faces of the five strangers standing around the bed he was in. He yawned as a rumble of hunger moved across his stomach.

"How do you feel?" James asked his patient.

"Groggy," the boy replied. "That, plus a little nauseous. Was I drugged?"

"Yes," James told him. "How much do you remember?"

"Not a whole lot. I...was working by myself in the computer lab when I suddenly realized I wasn't alone anymore. I looked up from the keyboard as a group of strange men rushed into the lab." He paused, hesitating a moment. "You five men aren't the guys I saw. They were Mexican, I think. Anyway, they all spoke Spanish." He licked his dry lips. "May I have some water?"

"I'll get it," Hahn volunteered.

As Hahn went to fulfill the boy's request, James urged Bobby Pearce to continue. "Go on, then. After these men entered the computer lab, what then?"

"This short guy—he may have had a mustache—he came forward and told me in English that my father had been injured in some kind of unspecified accident and that he and his friends were there to take me to him."

Hahn returned with a glass of water that the boy gratefully accepted. "Thanks." He raised his head off the pillow far enough to allow him to sip the liquid. He managed two full swallows, then passed the glass over to James and lowered his head to the pillow again. "Much better."

"How did you react to what the man said?" James asked.

"I was suspicious, not only because the man's story sounded phony, but also because the rest of the men with him did absolutely nothing to conceal their weapons.

"Anyway, although they were between me and the door out of the lab, I thought if I was lucky, I might be able to jump from my chair and run from the room before they could stop me." He frowned. "I only took a couple of steps before they caught me.

"One of the Mexicans gripped me by the shoulder and yanked my wrist away from my body. That's when I saw the short man coming at me with a needle in his hand, and then I felt this pain stabbing me in the arm." He reached his right fingertips to his left deltoid. "It's still sore. Anyhow, I felt the pain and—and the next thing I know I'm waking up in a strange bed and answering questions from somebody I don't even know. Who are you guys?"

"Let's just say we're the guys who kept you from taking a Mexican hayride," McCarter said.

Bobby Pearce persisted. "So you rescued me. That still doesn't tell me who you are."

"I'm afraid that's all we can tell you about ourselves, young man," Katz apologized. "The important thing is for you to know that you are safe."

"Does that mean you're with the government?"

"Again," Katz answered politely, "that is privileged information."

Concern showed on the boy's face. "What about my father? Was he really injured in an accident?"

"Not exactly," Manning confessed.

"What then? The Mexicans?"

"Yes," Manning said. Before Bobby Pearce awoke, Phoenix Force had agreed to be as honest as possible with the boy. "They kidnapped your father."

"But why? Dad's never hurt anyone in his life."

"That's not why we believe they singled him out," James admitted. "As far as we can figure out, your father was abducted in order for the group to collect some sort of ransom."

The boy shook his head back and forth on the pillow. "Not my dad. It just doesn't add up."

Katz disagreed. "It does if the men responsible for kidnapping your father thought he was tied in with a dramatic breakthrough in America's Strategic Defense Initiative program—a breakthrough that could advance SDI's timetable by more than a decade."

Uneasily, Bobby Pearce sat up in bed. "You guys are definitely with the government. What you're telling me is strictly top-level stuff. Only a handful of people are aware of the SDI breakthrough."

"Just as long as only a few people know your dad's not the real muscle behind it," McCarter said. "The Mexicans grabbed the wrong person."

The boy's shoulders slumped. "Yeah, that's right. But what happens when they discover their mistake?"

"Maybe they won't," James said. "In the meantime, we want to assure you that we will do everything within our power to secure your father's release."

"I can see how it was," Bobby Pearce decided. "Going after me in the computer lab was just a fluke. They could have used me to try and force dad to play ball."

"Only now they don't enjoy that luxury," Hahn pointed out. "We have you tucked safely out of reach of the kidnappers, and that's how it's going to stay."

The telephone rang in the next room, and Katz excused himself to answer it, making his departure just as Hahn revealed his admiration for the articles Bobby Pearce had written on advanced computer programming techniques.

Katzenelenbogen closed the bedroom door behind him and crossed to the phone.

"Yes?" he answered.

An operator explained that she was placing a person-to-person call to a Mr. Gray. Katz identified himself as the party in question, then waited for the call to be put through. He heard a click on the line and then Hal Brognola's familiar voice.

"Good afternoon, Mr. Gray," Brognola said. "How are you and your salesmen enjoying California?"

Although the Stony Man honcho was speaking from a secure telephone line at his end, the super Fed could not be sure that the conversation would not be overheard at Katz's end. It was unlikely that anyone within the hotel was listening in, but there was no reason to take any chances.

"My salesmen are doing fine," Katz said.

"Are you going to be able to close the big account soon?"

"Not really. We do have the smaller account wrapped up though," Katz stated, referring to the fact that Bobby Pearce was now in Phoenix Force's custody.

"Excellent." Brognola's sense of relief came over the line loud and clear.

"About that big account?"

"Yes?"

"Part of the problem is that other salesmen are interested in landing it."

"Previous competition?"

"Our friends from the Bahamas."

"I see," Brognola said, pausing to digest Katz's reference to MERGE. "That certainly does put your present situation in perspective, Mr. Gray. By the way, since I know that the major account is so important to your sales team, you should be aware that other companies are going to get a chance to bid on the contract."

"Our competitors who are always in a hurry?" the Israeli guessed.

"That's right," Brognola verified, knowing Katz meant the Russians. "As a matter of fact, your competitors have been offered the account by your Bahamian friends."

"How much?"

"Rumor has it at one hundred shares."

"Think they'll go for it?" Katz asked.

"I think they will. It's a chance in a million."

"I see," Katz said, knowing that from what Brognola implied, the Soviets had been offered Robert Pearce for a sum that could go as high as one hundred million dollars. "That many shares changing hands is sure to draw attention. If the deal goes through, maybe you could let me know about it?"

"I'd be happy to, Mr. Gray. Oh, and that information you wanted about the singers you saw last night?" Katz had requested a background check on the four men who had attacked the Phoenix duo at the Pearce home.

"I'm listening," Katz said.

"All four have been making records for a long time," Brognola informed the Phoenix team's commander. "But as far as we can tell, they've always been solo artists."

"Yes, well, perhaps they were performing a one-night stand for the competition?" Katz suggested. "At any rate, please keep in touch."

"I will. Give my best to your sales team."

"I'll do that."

"Good. Speak to you later, Mr. Gray."

12

Major Viktor Kulik threw caution to the wind and actually embraced the dreaded Captain Oleg Lensky. Kulik's face was painted with a genuine smile for the first time in weeks. The major bear-hugged his colleague for a few seconds longer, then broke away and allowed his cheerful grin to grow even larger.

"Do you know why I did that, Lensky?" Kulik asked.

A suspicious Lensky went for broke. "You're beginning to miss your wife too much?"

"My wife? Ridiculous! No, you fool. I embraced you because at long last our troubles are over."

Wondering if the major might indeed be going mad, Lensky asked, "Does that mean the communiqué you just deciphered was good news?"

"More than that, Lensky. It's our ticket out of this mess concerning Pearce. Our key out of jail."

"The Collegium has found someone else to blame?" the captain guessed hopefully.

"There was no need for them to do so, Lensky, for the people who successfully kidnapped Pearce have agreed to sell him to us."

"What do you mean?"

"Our consulate here in Los Angeles was contacted and the offer was made." He checked the time on his watch. "We must leave within the hour. We are to drive to the main entrance of the Carson Mall and wait to be contacted. They will recognize us because you will be cleaning the windshield of our automobile. What will happen after that I do not know."

"What is the price they are asking for Pearce?"

"Your guess is almost as good as mine," Kulik answered. "No set amount for the ransom has been given. However, our orders are explicit: we are to agree to whatever financial arrangements Pearce's captors demand and not quibble about price. We must promise whatever is necessary to get Robert Pearce in our possession."

"CLEAN IT AGAIN."

"It's already clean."

"Lensky!" Kulik warned. "I don't care if you polish a hole right through the glass, clean the damn windshield again."

Lensky mumbled something rude under his breath and began spraying liquid cleaner on the windshield again. He was reaching for the paper towel to wipe the glass dry when a jet-black Buick Electra pulled up and parked alongside the Soviets' Dodge Diplomat. The Buick's passenger door opened, and a man wearing a cool summer suit stepped out of the car.

"Nice job," the summer-suited Hispanic observed, noting the way the Diplomat's windshield gleamed. "Maybe you could do the same for my car sometime? What do you think?"

Kulik, who had been listening with the window down, emerged from the Dodge. "He thinks, as I do, that it is time to talk business. We have met with you as instructed. Now what?"

"You are the top man with your company?"

Kulik nodded. "If there is a payment to be made for merchandise, then I am the one to authorize it."

"Good," the Mexican said. "After I determine you are not armed, you will get into the back seat of the car I arrived in and take a ride."

The Soviet major indicated Lensky. "And my associate?"

"Will remain here with me. If we discover that you have tried to lure us into a trap," he lifted open the front of his sports jacket so Kulik could see a gun, "then your associate will die."

"Fair enough," Kulik said, ignoring Lensky's wide-eyed look. "But you must believe from our end that we are approaching this transaction with the best of intentions."

"That remains to be seen," said the man with the gun.

Kulik was frisked for weapons and then led to the rear door of the nearby Electra. The door popped open and the major climbed in, exchanging a final glance with his nervous captain as the door was closed. Immediately, the driver of the Buick got the car rolling, slowly leaving Lensky and his unwelcome companion behind.

"I don't believe we've met," the middle-aged Hispanic man next to Kulik said. "My name is Armando."

"Viktor," Kulik supplied, somewhat reluctantly shaking hands with his fellow passenger.

"How pleased I am to see you could make today's appointment, Viktor."

"I made a special effort because the firm I represent may be interested in something you have to sell."

"Yes," Torres-Quinteros said. "The commodity you seek uses the name of Robert Pearce."

"Precisely what we have been looking for," Kulik confirmed. "But it is difficult to pay for an item when the terms for making that purchase are unknown."

"And that is why we are traveling up and down the aisles of the shopping mall's parking lot together. It gives us an excellent opportunity to discuss the terms of the sale."

"Simply put, then, Armando... how much do you want in exchange for Robert Pearce?"

"Originally, we had planned on asking fifty million dollars."

Like a dying teakettle, air whistled between the major's teeth.

"But that was before, Viktor," the MERGE boss reported, "before we discovered that you were also interested in obtaining Senor Pearce. You did suffer the loss of three of your men Friday night, I believe?"

"I will neither confirm nor deny such a loss."

"Yes, Viktor, I did not think you would do so. But to return to monetary matters. As I said, we had planned on asking fifty million dollars for our prize, but that was when we believed the American government would be our only buyers. Having a new customer enter the sales arena alters the situation considerably."

"And means you can increase the asking price for Pearce and still expect to get it. Again, how much are we talking about?"

"One hundred million dollars."

Kulik made a poor showing at disguising his surprise. "That's an absurd sum to ask for a single man!"

Torres-Quinteros shrugged. "An ordinary man, perhaps, but that certainly doesn't describe Senor Pearce or his abilities as a superlative computer programmer. I don't imagine that you would have come to see me today if you and those you represent did not agree.

"Forgive me if I say so, Viktor, but your people have not exactly carried the torch into the age of the computer. If the technology has not been successfully purchased or stolen, then your computer scientists do not possess it. Which is why paying what we want for Robert Pearce is still a bargain."

"You must show me another time, Armando," Kulik said, "this dictionary wherein 'bargain' is defined as such. However, I have been authorized to agree to your terms. How would you like the payment to be made?"

Torres-Quinteros handed the major an envelope. "Inside you will find the account number for a bank in Mexico City. Once it has been determined that the appropriate monetary amount has been deposited, your consulate will be notified as to where to accept delivery of Senor Pearce."

"And what's to prevent you from running off with both Pearce and the money?" Kulik asked.

"I am first and foremost a businessman, Viktor. The global reputation of your KGB is quite familiar to me. I have no wish to spend the remaining years of my life looking over my shoulder. To take your money and then cheat you would be suicide on my part. I want to live a long life, to see my grandchildren. No, deposit the one hundred million dollars into the account, Viktor, and you shall have Robert Pearce. You have my word."

"How long am I to be given to arrange for the deposit?" Kulik asked.

"Six hours."

"Impossible," the major protested. "That's not enough time."

"Believe me, Viktor, it is. With the resources you have access to, you could have the funds into the account in Mexico in half that time. Six hours. Agreed?"

Frustrated, Major Kulik sighed. "Six hours."

Then the driver brought the car to a halt in front of Kulik's Dodge.

"It's been a pleasure doing business with you, Viktor," the MERGE leader said. "Goodbye."

"A pleasure," Kulik lied, then stepped from the car as Rinaldo Orona-Torres, the man guarding Lensky, reclaimed his place in the front seat of the Buick.

"How did it go, Uncle?" Orona-Torres inquired.

"The Soviets have no choice. They will pay what we are asking for Pearce and have agreed to do so within the next six hours."

"And in the meantime, Uncle?"

"We must do two things," the man told his nephew. "First, I want you to take the photo of Bobby Pearce that we discovered in his father's wallet and have the picture copied. Then I want it distributed to all of our contacts throughout the city. There are plenty of hungry people in Los Angeles. Issue a reward of ten thousand dollars for the boy."

"As you wish, Uncle. And the second thing?"

"That I will take care of. I will inform the Americans that they may also purchase Pearce for one hundred million dollars."

"But suppose the United States agrees to pay, Uncle? What then? You've already promised Pearce to the Soviets. They can't both have him."

"True," Torres-Quinteros said with a laugh. "But the Americans don't know that."

13

Colonel Yakov Katzenelenbogen hung up the telephone.

"That was Hal again," Katz said.

"We knew it wasn't room service," McCarter offered. "What's the good word?"

"For starters," the Israeli began, "an extensive security net has been lowered over the entire Los Angeles area." Bobby Pearce was watching television in an adjoining room, so Katz was able to speak freely. "Nothing is being overlooked. All bus and train stations, as well as local airports, are under strict surveillance. With the lid that's been clamped on all flights departing from LAX, MERGE couldn't get Robert Pearce on a jet out of L.A. if they had him disguised as carry-on luggage."

"How about the highways leading out of California?" James asked.

"They're also under wraps," Katz said. "Emergency inspection stations have been established on every major and secondary route that MERGE might possibly use to transport Pearce from the region. Strongest emphasis in this direction is being placed north of San Diego on Interstate 5. All vehicles going south toward Mexico are subject to a search by INS officials. At the border into Tijuana, they're making travelers do everything but fill out a credit application."

"What's the likelihood of MERGE heading north with Pearce?" Manning questioned. "San Francisco International Airport could get Bobby's father out of the country just as well as LAX."

"San Francisco is undergoing essentially the same security precautions that have been implemented here," Katz said.

"Good," Hahn concluded. "Such restrictions on travel will certainly hamper MERGE's ability to spirit their prisoner from the U.S."

"It also encourages MERGE to speed up its deal with the Soviets," Manning said, "so that the KGB will have the headache of getting Pearce to Moscow."

"If the deal with the Soviets goes through," Katz interjected.

"Don't tell me our friends in Red are backing out?" James said.

"They're going through with it, all right," Katz admitted. "Hal reported that a new account with a bank in Mexico City has been receiving substantially large deposits during the past couple of hours. So far, the deposits total eighty-seven million dollars, just thirteen shy of what MERGE is asking for Pearce."

"What makes you think the deal will go sour, then?" McCarter asked. "Surely if the Soviets are putting out that kind of money, they're definitely going to want something to show for it."

"Of course," Katz said. "But that doesn't explain why the U.S. government has also been offered Robert Pearce under basically the same conditions as those given the Soviets."

"Sounds like MERGE is trying to sell Pearce twice," Hahn suggested.

"Something like that," agreed Katz. "In any case, Hal has supplied me with all of the details we need to proceed. MERGE wants to meet with an official representative from Washington. That's what we're going to give them." He turned to James. "Calvin, I want you to pose as our man from D.C."

"You got it," James said.

"Gary," Katz continued, "you'll be with Calvin as his driver. Neither of you are to be armed. As much as I'd like to throttle our MERGE contacts, we can't risk it without putting Robert Pearce's life in more danger than it already is in."

"Right," James said. "We'll just play it by ear and see what MERGE has in mind."

"That's what I want." Katz nodded. "The meeting with MERGE is scheduled to take place at a nearby shopping mall in—" he glanced at his watch "—ninety minutes. Up until now, it looked like MERGE's interest in this whole business with Pearce was purely financial, but there's always the chance they've got something else up their sleeve. Whatever their intent, when the meeting with MERGE goes down, Karl and I will be stationed close enough to come in fighting if necessary."

"Okay," McCarter said to Katz. "Calvin and Gary meet with MERGE. You and Karl work backup. Where's that leave me?"

The Israeli's eyes went to the door to the room where Bobby Pearce was, then back to the Briton. "Guess."

"Cheers," McCarter grumbled.

THERE WAS NOTHING Calvin James liked about Armando Torres-Quinteros, and that included the MERGE boss's taste in clothing. What James disliked most, though, was his adversary's attitude. Armando Torres-Quinteros reeked of arrogance; he wore it proudly like the cheap cologne he obviously bought by the liter.

Manning was left under the watchful eye of a MERGE underling, while James was frisked for concealed weapons and then invited for a ride in the back seat of Torres-Quinteros's car. The two men introduced themselves and then shook hands. As the Buick they were in slowly rode up and down the aisles of the shopping mall's parking lot, they got down to business.

"I am pleased that you could join me, Senor Blue," the MERGE honcho spoke, addressing James by the name the Phoenix commando had supplied. "Hopefully, once we have had the opportunity to talk, we will reach a mutually satisfying agreement."

"Our concern is for the safe return of Robert Pearce," James stated. "That's it in a nutshell. What's it going to take for that to happen?"

"I admire your straightforward approach, Senor Blue. It will save us much time."

"Glad to hear it. Now, how much are you asking for Pearce?"

"One hundred million dollars."

James feigned astonishment. "Whoa, hold on there, Armando. You're talking one hell of a bundle. What makes you think Robert Pearce is worth that much to us?"

"If he wasn't, you wouldn't be here," Torres-Quinteros countered. "Robert Pearce is worth anything we want to ask for him and you know it."

James did not deny the charge. "And exactly how do you propose that such a substantial amount of money change hands?"

"Simple. After I return you to your driver, you will arrange to have the money transferred to a bank in Mexico City." He gave James an envelope. "Because I was sure you would meet our price for Senor Pearce, I took the liberty of opening a new account with the bank. The address of the bank and the number of that account are contained in the envelope."

James slipped the packet of information into the pocket of his suit. "You've thought of everything."

Armando Torres-Quinteros smiled. "That is why I am in a position to issue demands that your government must accept."

"Robert Pearce has not been heard from in over forty-eight hours. What proof do we have that he's even alive?"

"Would I be attempting to sell him to you if he wasn't?"

"You tell me."

"Rest assured, Senor Blue, Robert Pearce is healthy and comfortable. All his needs are being seen to."

Except his freedom, James thought. "What about a good faith gesture on your part? If the American government is prepared to pay what you're asking for

Pearce, are you willing to take me to see him so that I can verify he's as healthy as you say?"

"What you propose is absolutely out of the question. Besides, I would think that saving Robert Pearce from the Russians would be proof enough of our good faith. You cannot pretend you don't know what I'm talking about?"

"There were three Soviet agents altogether. One had his throat slit and the other two were shot."

"Precisely. And they were killed while in the process of abducting Senor Pearce at gunpoint. If not for our timely intervention, it would have become necessary to forward Senor Pearce's mail to Moscow."

"I'm certain the President would honor such heroism with a medal."

"I prefer cash."

"Tell me," James asked, "if you know the Soviets are interested in Pearce, then why not try to do business with them?"

"I do not trade with Communists," Torres-Quinteros lied. "Senor Pearce is an American and should remain here at home. I have told you the price for letting him do so. Do you anticipate any difficulties?"

"None off the top of my head."

"Let us keep it that way, Senor Blue."

The cellular phone in front of the MERGE leader signaled an incoming call. Torres-Quinteros answered the phone. A one-sided conversation ensued in which he did most of the listening. The call was over in less than a minute.

"Excuse me," Torres-Quinteros apologized as he hung up. "Where were we?"

"I was saying there should be no problem in depositing the money to your account in Mexico City as requested."

"And once I know that the deposit has been made in full, you will be informed as to where Senor Pearce may be found."

The car pulled to a stop close to where James and Manning had originally parked. James saw that his Canadian friend was still being guarded by Armando Torres-Quinteros's flunkie. James opened the door to get out.

"One more thing, Senor Blue."

"Yes?"

"Be forewarned. If your government is less than honest in its intentions to make the promised payment, you will never see Senor Pearce again. On the other hand, if the U.S. deposit is made by midnight tonight, then I shall feel obliged to include a bonus."

"Oh?" James had no idea what Torres-Quinteros was driving at. "What kind of bonus?"

"We are prepared to throw in Senor Pearce's son, Bobby, for good measure."

A cold chill of dread knifed through his stomach as James remembered the phone call Torres-Quinteros had received.

"Bobby Pearce?" James said. "Does that mean you have the boy, too?"

What Alvin Drand liked most about working at the Holder Arms Hotel were the guests. Impeccably groomed and always flashing his warm and ready smile, Drand continually distinguished himself as one of the hardest working employees on the hotel's staff. Drand's job at the Holder Arms was that of a floater, which meant that he put his many talents to work on a variety of tasks.

A leaky bathroom sink in Room 716? Send for Alvin Drand. A TV on the blink in Room 314? Get Drand to fix it. The ice machine on the eleventh floor produced nothing but puddles? Put Drand on it right away.

In his five years at the Holder Arms, Alvin Drand had proved himself to be an invaluable asset to his employers. Gripe about working holidays? Not Drand. Complain about overtime? No way. When extra hours were available, he was the first in line to get them. To his credit, Drand never once made a fuss about any irregularity that popped up on his work schedule. If the Holder Arms needed him, then Alvin Drand was sure to be there. It was as simple as that.

Almost.

While his employers thought Drand's remarkable dedication to the hotel was the result of fortunate hiring on their part, the truth of the matter was that Alvin Drand actually had more important things on his mind when checking the air conditioner in 227 or fluffing the pillows in 409. His employers thought he was working for them, but as far as Drand was concerned, he was working for himself.

Alvin Drand was a thief, which was why he liked the hotel's guests so much. After all they had contributed to his financial well-being through the years, it would have been wrong for him not to feel grateful.

Drand's system was simple. He never stole more than he could carry in a single trip to the trunk of his car. He never stole from the same floor twice within a six-month period, and whatever he did steal was always something he could sell.

Rings and watches were his specialty, the easiest to move. In five years, he had lifted enough jewelry to stock a pawnshop. Credit cards were another hot item. One minute with a guest's wallet and he was in business. Drand would remove a single credit card and leave the rest alone; that way as much as a week could pass before the lost card was missed.

Valued by his employers, a favorite among his coworkers and popular with the guests, Drand was never considered a suspect in any of the thefts. That Alvin Drand, pride and joy of the Holder Arms, would be involved in such foul deeds was unthinkable. And so Drand's career as a thief prospered unchecked.

But the rings, watches and credit cards meant nothing without an outlet to dispose of the stolen property. Fortunately, Drand had established a limited number of reliable and discreet buyers who were always pleased to offer him fair value for whatever merchandise he had on hand. They were Drand's friends and he was theirs. And whenever the opportunity cropped up to do a favor for one another, neither side hesitated.

And that was how Alvin Drand happened on his latest gold mine. While exchanging three credit cards and a couple of diamond rings for cash, Drand's buyer mentioned that certain unnamed parties were scouting around town for a runaway kid, and there was a ten thousand dollar reward for anyone who could locate the boy.

Drand asked for the runaway's description and was given a photo and a phone number.

"Hang onto the picture, Alvin," the buyer advised. "Ten grand ain't chicken feed. Besides, you might get lucky."

The poker-faced Drand took one look at the photo and calmly slipped the picture out of sight. He said his goodbyes, then hurried back to the Holder Arms, his heart racing like a steam engine going downhill. *Ten thousand dollars!*

Drand instantly recognized the boy in the photograph—the kid was staying on the ninth floor, Room 906. Drand had been on his way to the front desk late Saturday night when the boy in the picture was physically carried into the hotel. The kid was asleep at the time, dead to the world, but Drand had made it his business to see what the boy looked like. And now it turned out that his curiosity was going to pay off in a very big way.

Back at the Holder Arms, Drand first made sure that the guests in 906 had not checked out. They had not. Then he went to one of the pay phones in the main lobby and called the number that was the key to the reward money. Giving his name, Drand told the voice he had some information about the runaway. He was told to expect a visitor within the hour. Drand gave his description to the man on the other end and then went to the hotel's underground parking lot to wait.

A Mexican in his early thirties soon approached Drand. "You are Alvin Drand?" the man asked.

Drand nodded, noting as he did that the man wore a tailored suit with baggy trousers. The two Hispanics accompanying him were similarly attired. All three men regarded him with fish-eyed stares that Drand found disconcerting. Ten grand was ten grand, though, and he was not about to get cold feet.

"I phoned," Drand said.

"About the boy in this picture?" The man doing the talking produced a copy of the photo Drand already had. "He is here at the hotel?"

"Upstairs in Room 906," Drand answered.

"Is he alone?"

"No, there's somebody with him. One guy. There were four others, but while I was waiting for you to arrive, I saw them get into cars in the lot and leave."

"How long ago was that?"

Drand checked his Timex. "Twenty minutes ago, I guess. Listen, what about the reward money for tipping you off? The person I got the photo from said ten thousand dollars was being offered. I've done my share. How about paying me?"

The stern-faced Hispanic held up the briefcase he was carrying. "You'll be paid, but only after we're sure the boy is really inside the room you say. We would like to get to him before his four friends return. Lead the way and we will follow."

Convinced he would forfeit the reward money if he did not comply with the order, Drand turned and led the three men between the rows of parked cars to the nearby elevator. He pushed the call button and stepped aside as the elevator doors opened. The lift was deserted. Drand and the men he was leading got in. The doors closed and the elevator began to rise.

"Where'd the kid run away from?" Drand asked, making conversation as they rode upstairs. "His folks hire you to track him down or something, is that it?"

"Please, what you ask is unimportant," the Hispanic carrying the briefcase said. "All you need to know is that we have been sent for the boy. Nothing more."

"Hey," Drand quickly backed away from the subject, "no problem. You don't want to tell me, that's fine. Just settle my account and I'm history. Deal?"

The elevator stopped and seemed to drop into place as its doors opened on the ninth floor. Once they were off, Drand immediately pointed his finger to the right.

"Straight down the hall and around the corner," the pride of the Holder Arms said. "906...you can't miss it. Now, about my money?"

"Is there somewhere I can pay you in private?" the man with the briefcase wanted to know. I wouldn't want our business transaction to be interrupted. Do you understand?"

"Yeah, sure," Drand said, louder than necessary, wanting to kick himself in the ass for not being able to control his nervousness. He jerked his thumb to the left. "There's a utility room halfway down the corridor."

"Is it locked?"

Drand nodded. "But I have a key."

The Hispanic motioned to Drand. "After you."

Drand fumbled for the key and started down the hall. "We'll have to make this snappy," he said, reaching the utility room and unlocking the door. "I'm not supposed to have access to the place."

"This won't take long," the man with Drand's reward promised.

Drand opened the door and both men entered the tiny room. The stinging smell of disinfectant brought tears to Drand's eyes. His knees were shaking. He pulled the door shut and switched on an overhead light.

The man with Drand threw his briefcase onto a shelf and opened it. Drand gasped in shock at what he saw.

"Oh, God, no man, wait, don't, I—"

Drand never finished his sentence as the ugly black gun in the Mexican's hand coughed twice and sent Drand stumbling to the floor. Fire burned holes through his stomach and side. His shirt felt sticky and wet. And warm. No sound came out when he screamed. The overhead light was dimming.

Alvin Drand's last thought was of someone touching his hand, prying open his fingers, reaching for his key. Reaching for his . . . Reaching . . .

15

"I was playing with my first computer when most kids my age were learning to ride a bicycle."

"Did you ever learn to ride one?" McCarter asked.

"We took the training wheels off last month," Bobby Pearce replied with a trace of a smile turning up the corners of his mouth. "I don't know how it is in England, but here a kid's first driving experience usually comes sitting on his father's lap behind the wheel of the family car. That's how it was with me and computers.

"I'd sit with Dad and play what he called the 'keyboard game.' He'd show me how to do something and I'd repeat it. Right from the start I was pretty good at it, and I don't mean simply duplicating some computer trick I'd seen performed, either. The concepts behind what I was doing at the keyboard came to me naturally. I didn't have to force them.

"Dad said I had an aptitude for computers that would have developed with or without his encouragement. It just lucked out that Dad was adept with computers and could guide me along."

"Yet with all your father's experience, you're better at it than he is," McCarter observed. "When did that happen?"

"Three years ago. Dad was working on a project that had him stumped. He'd been approaching the problem from every angle but the right one."

"But you set him straight," the Englishman guessed.

"It was an accident," the youthful computer genius said. "Dad had been at it for fifteen hours or more and decided to take a break. While he ran downstairs to fix himself a sandwich, I happened to pass by the computer terminal he'd been working at. The program he was trying to write was stretched out on the monitor screen from top to bottom. I looked at the screen and, well, it was almost like my dad's program jumped right out at me. I studied it carefully, and by the time Dad came back upstairs, I thought I'd found the solution to his problem. It turned out that I was right."

"And I suppose after that things progressed to the point that you and your dad became a regular team?"

"Close to it," the boy admitted. "But at the start, we kept that a secret. Dad explained that some of his associates wouldn't take a kid seriously, not to mention the fact that I'd make them look like they'd just stepped out of school. And he was right. When we finally did go public, at least so far as the DoD was concerned, more than one of Dad's colleagues complained and tried to have me barred from working with my father on any defense-related projects."

"What happened?" McCarter questioned.

Bobby Pearce chuckled. "One of the men got an early retirement and the other two spend most of their time testing seawater samples in Guam."

"Serves 'em right."

McCarter rose from his chair and crossed to where a bucket of ice and several cans of Coke were sitting on a table. The Briton selected a can and held it up.

"Fancy a drink?"

"No, thanks."

McCarter opened the can and poured the cola into a glass, topping the drink off with a couple of ice cubes. Taking the half-empty can with him, he carried everything back to his chair and sat down.

"That's better." McCarter drained most of the Coke in a single swallow.

"These people who have my dad—" the boy began once McCarter was settled "—can your friends handle them?"

"The meeting they went to is not supposed to lead to any fireworks. Even if it did, though, they'd know what to do."

"But you don't think there'll be any shooting?"

"No," McCarter said. "The bunch holding your dad want to make as much money as they can before turning him loose. Starting a gunfight with the U.S. representatives brought in to negotiate with them won't do their bankbooks any good. That's why they're likely to limit their activities this time round to a show of strength and not much else."

"Does that mean they're all talk?"

"Afraid not, Bobby. I wish I could tell you otherwise, but the truth is, your father's abductors are cold-blooded killers. If your dad's health wasn't important to them, it would probably already be too late for my friends and I to help him."

"How come somebody from England is working for the Americans? Or the rest of your friends? From what I've been able to determine, only one out of five is really from the States. I thought you had to be U.S. citizens to work for the government."

"There are exceptions to every set of rules," McCarter said matter-of-factly. "But that's even assuming we're employed by the American government."

"Aren't you?"

"Can you tell me everything about your breakthrough for the Strategic Defense Initiative?" the Cockney commando countered.

"Of course not."

"I'm in the same boat. What me and my mates do is what we do, and the fewer who know about it, the more we like it. I'd like to quote you chapter and verse, but I can't."

"I understand," the boy said. "We all have our little secrets."

"Ain't it the truth."

McCarter drank the last of his cola and quickly refilled his glass as Bobby pointed to the Browning Hi-Power the Briton wore.

"Do you ever take off your gun?" he asked.

The Briton smiled. "Sometimes when I take a bath."

McCarter's genial attitude vanished in an instant as his battle-honed sense of hearing caught the sound of a key being inserted into the lock of the door to their suite.

Immediately, the Phoenix lion withdrew his Browning, rising from his chair as he ordered Bobby, "Go into the next room and close the door after you. Push anything you can find up against it to block it and don't come out until I tell you it's safe. Move!"

But before Bobby Pearce could obey the command, the front door of the suite slammed open and terror swept into the room in the form of three MERGE gunmen.

The first killer through the doorway charged in a rush for McCarter, ignoring or not seeing the 9 mm semiauto in the Briton's fist. That oversight proved fatal as McCarter fired, unleashing a blazing two-round burst that collided with the attacking MERGE thug at near point-blank range.

Part of the hood's head disintegrated into a blossoming shower of red that shot bits of scalp and much of the killer's pompadour hairstyle toward the ceiling. Shot number two ripped out the tough's throat in a hot, bloody spray.

But the corpse refused to die and continued its charge, the fading life in its legs carrying it forward, transporting the dying lump of flesh straight into McCarter's arms. As McCarter pushed the dead man aside, the second MERGE gunman attacked; he rushed at the Phoenix pro with a full body tackle.

Air spilled from McCarter's lungs as both he and his Mexican foe hit the floor. The MERGE gunman's weapon went flying. Ditto McCarter's Browning. The Londoner caught an image of Bobby Pearce fleeing into the room next door, and then the British powerhouse was caught in a fight for his life.

Bare knuckles loomed over McCarter's face, aiming for his jaw. The Phoenix commando extended his arms, twisting out of the way. The clenched hand struck the empty carpet.

McCarter tucked his knees into his chest and kicked, his feet connecting with the Mexican's stomach, causing the MERGE hood to groan in pain as he was propelled through the air, crash-landing to the floor on the seat of his pleated pants.

The Briton pulled himself into an upright position, his teeth bared in an angry smile. His Hi-Power was off to the left, his enemy's revolver not far from it. There was no time to safely reach for either.

The MERGE thug climbed to his feet, eyes full of rage and spitting venom.

"I'm going to kill you," McCarter's would-be executioner promised.

"No way, Jose," the British commando snapped back.

Sharp steel flashed in the MERGE killer's right hand as he lunged, leaping across the carpeted space that separated him from McCarter. Rather than withdraw, McCarter squared off against his adversary, attacking with an outward circle block that forced the enemy's knife away from the Englishman's body.

Pushing out on his opponent's wrist, McCarter locked the Mexican's elbow open with a palm heel strike of his left hand. The Briton's fingers dug deeply into the flesh of the elbow, causing the Mexican's knife to cut jerking patterns through the air. McCarter's right fist shot up and out, driving a solid punch to the side of the MERGE hit man's head.

The killer groaned and staggered. McCarter clamped his right hand over the wrist that held the knife, turning it inward and driving the point of the seven-inch blade straight for the Mexican's belly. The MERGE goon had no choice but to relinquish control of the dagger. His fingers opened and dropped the blade.

"Party's over, sunshine," McCarter said, releasing the killer's wrist, and then sending his fist in a rock-hard blow to the Mexican's nose.

Blood spurted beneath McCarter's fingers as the man from MERGE stumbled back two steps and sank to his knees, his labored breathing decorating the carpet with red each time he exhaled. His hand vanished into the rear pocket of his trousers and reappeared holding another knife.

"I slice you to ribbons," the killer blubbered through his ruined proboscis.

"Some other time," the Briton suggested.

Grabbing a lamp off a nearby table, McCarter tore its electrical cord from the wall. He brought the base of the lamp down and up in a violent swing. The Briton's improvised club collided with the MERGE hood's head and shattered, caving in the killer's skull as though it were made of soft cheese. The south-of-the-border switchblade fell from the dead man's hand as the Mexican's body slumped forward onto its face.

"Next year, the Ashes," McCarter said, dropping what was left of the lamp to the floor as he searched for and found his fallen Browning.

Expecting sounds of a struggle, but hearing nothing, McCarter rushed into the next room to check on Bobby Pearce. The room was deserted; neither the boy nor the third MERGE gunman was there. An open window beckoned from the far end of the room. McCarter ran to it and cautiously leaned out for a look.

The window opened onto a rusting fire escape. There was no one on the stairs leading to the ground. But two flights overhead, McCarter could see that

Bobby was outdistancing the last of the MERGE killers by a gap that was rapidly closing. Then the boy lost his footing and his lead evaporated. The MERGE tough reached out and snagged the prize he was chasing.

Hi-Power in hand, McCarter snarled like an unleashed tiger and jumped through the window to the fire escape. The metal staircase shook with his additional weight. He clasped the iron banister and climbed.

Alerted by a noise from below, the MERGE mobster turned to confront the Briton's unexpected appearance. The killer aimed his gun and fired, the silenced weapon spewing a bullet that sparked off the railing next to McCarter's left wrist. McCarter kept climbing and the gunman drilled a neat little hole through the step McCarter was standing on.

"Bloody hell!" the Cockney combat veteran swore as he reached the tenth floor. With the killer using him for target practice and still maintaining his decisive hold on Bobby Pearce, McCarter's Browning was virtually useless.

Had he been going one-on-one with his MERGE adversary, McCarter would have had no problem bagging his opponent. The Englishman's skills with a handgun had earned him a position on Great Britain's shooting team. Only commitments to the SAS prevented McCarter from participating in the 1980 Olympic Games.

But having Bobby Pearce's safety to consider changed all that. Putting the boy in the middle of a firefight left McCarter at a definite disadvantage, and the MERGE tough knew it.

Not that Bobby Pearce was making things easy for his captor. Far from it. As Mexico's answer to Little Caesar tried to control the boy and shoot McCarter at the same time, the young computer genius was doing everything he could to break free of the Mexican's tenacious grip.

McCarter held his ground midway between the tenth and eleventh floors as another silenced slug occupied the space he was about to fill. One flight of metal steps separated him from his foe. While the Hispanic gunman was not setting records in the accuracy department, McCarter was not overly anxious to give the MERGE gangster any more chances to better his record.

"Come any closer and I shoot the boy!" the killer warned in heavily accented English.

"Let the kid go," McCarter returned without stepping around and onto the fire escape's landing. "Set him free."

"Ha, you must be crazy, man. The boy is my ticket out of here."

"The only ticket you've got is one with Boneyard stamped on it. Let the boy go and you have my word I won't shoot you."

The MERGE hood laughed again, although this time his nervousness showed. "The boy stays with me."

"Harm a hair on his head and you're dead."

The killer ignored McCarter's threat. "Move out into the open where I can see you."

McCarter hesitated.

"Now, I said!" the gunman repeated the command. "Step onto the landing or the boy's death is on your hands. Out now. Move!"

With the Browning hanging loosely by his side, McCarter slowly complied with the order and moved onto the landing, half expecting his MERGE adversary to shoot him on the spot. But the Mexican criminal held his fire, content for the moment to keep Bobby Pearce in front of him as a human shield.

The killer had the boy in a modified choke hold with his left arm, leaving his right arm free to dig the barrel of his gun into Bobby's side. McCarter had to admire the young man's courage. Although clearly in danger, the genuine fear in Bobby Pearce's eyes was tempered with an unmistakable look of determination.

"Drop your gun," the Mexican ordered, jabbing his weapon further into the boy's side for emphasis. "Do it now or, so help me, I will shoot."

McCarter believed the killer was desperate enough to follow through on his promise. He opened his fingers and allowed the Hi-Power to slip to the landing.

"Now what?" McCarter asked.

A smug expression of victory flashed across the MERGE thug's face. "Now, I kill you."

The killer swung his weapon away from the boy, which was when Bobby Pearce opened his mouth and sank his teeth into the Mexican's forearm. The MERGE mobster screamed. His shot went wild.

So did David McCarter.

Bounding up the steps of the fire excape as though he had been launched from a cannon, the London lion flew straight as an arrow toward his foe. The MERGE gunman shrieked when he saw McCarter coming, but the combination of the Briton's swift attack and the continuing distraction of Bobby Pearce prevented the frantic killer from doing anything to halt the Briton's advance.

The Hispanic hoodlum wrenched Bobby Pearce to the side and kicked at McCarter's face. McCarter stopped the foot by catching it by the ankle. He twisted and pulled it in an effort to throw his opponent off-balance. Swearing in Spanish, the killer was forced to let go of his gun and release his captive in order to remain upright.

Bobby Pearce fell to his knees on the fire escape's eleventh-floor landing. Using the waist-high metal railing at his back for support, the killer managed to pull his trapped leg free of McCarter's grip. Immediately, the MERGE goon shifted to the right, braced his foot against the Pearce boy's shoulder and shoved.

The kid toppled sideways, spilling into the yawning space beyond the barrier of the fire escape. Gravity reached out to reel him to the ground. McCarter lunged, diving for the boy, his fingers brushing against the fabric of the youngster's shirt. The boy continued to fall, helplessly windmilling his arms.

McCarter grabbed more of the fabric, bunching the shirt's cotton material into his hands. As he leaned back and pulled, the fabric started to tear. A pointed toe from the killer's shoe kicked the Briton in the side. He ignored the pain and tugged even harder on the boy.

Then Bobby Pearce's arms connected with the railing and his hands encircled the rusting banister in a shock-locked embrace of relief.

"I'm okay," the boy screamed to McCarter.

That was all the Phoenix Force pro needed to hear.

Opening the fist that had prevented the boy from plummeting to his death, McCarter leaped to the top of the landing before the MERGE hood could kick him back. The killer raised his fist to strike. McCarter doubled under the attack and staggered the Mexican with a devastating punch to the side of the head.

The killer moaned and shoved McCarter to the edge of the railing. Eleven floors below, Death invited McCarter for a cup and a natter.

"Piss off!" McCarter gritted through clenched teeth, grabbing the hood by the shoulders and then shifting his weight in reverse as he yanked the MERGE gangster forward toward the hotel building.

Crying hysterically at the top of his voice, the killer crashed headlong through the window of Room 1106. Glass shattered into a thousand knives. The squealing murderer strained his way into the suite, disappearing from the fire escape in a wet smear of blood.

McCarter kicked aside the shards of broken glass from the window frame and followed the Mexican hit man. The killer was thrashing upon the floor, screaming words that were no longer human. A severed jugular squirted rivers of red all over the carpet. Dying fingers sought to stem the precious tide. The bleeding man shuddered and died, his life draining onto the floor.

McCarter turned away from his dead MERGE adversary and crossed to the window to return to Bobby Pearce just as the boy was preparing to enter the room.

"Uh-uh," McCarter stopped him. "You don't want to see this. Trust me." The Cockney climbed through the window and back onto the fire escape. "We'll go back down the way we came up, only under happier circumstances. Are you okay?"

Bobby Pearce nodded. "Thanks for saving me after that guy tried putting me into orbit."

McCarter returned the compliment. "Thanks for taking a chunk out of his arm when it did the most good."

"Best meal I ever had," the boy grinned, wiping his mouth with the back of his hand. "That creep actually tried to kill me. What a rat."

"Yeah," McCarter agreed. "A regular cutup."

16

Calvin James was almost afraid to knock on the door when he and the remaining Phoenix Force members returned from their meeting with MERGE.

"If something's happened to David and the boy," James informed his companions, "I'll probably find Armando Torres-Quinteros and kick that dude's ass inside out."

James knocked firmly on the door—three quick taps with his knuckles, a four-second pause and then two more knocks.

They waited until finally a voice that each of the men recognized filtered through the door. "Who's there?"

"Open up," James answered. "It's us."

The lock was thrown clear, and McCarter opened the door to his friends. "Hi."

James was the first to enter. "Man, are we glad to see—oh, shit . . . I knew it. What the hell happened?"

Propped against the wall in one corner of the suite were a pair of dead MERGE mobsters. Pieces of the broken lamp that McCarter had used as a weapon were strewn about the floor.

"We had visitors," the Englishman said.

"Where's Bobby?" Katz inquired.

"Here," the boy announced, entering the room as he dried his wet hair with a towel. "I was cleaning up."

"Looks like you aren't the only one," Manning observed. "Can't say I'm surprised, though."

"When did they hit you?" Hahn asked.

"Close to thirty minutes after you left for the meeting," the Briton replied. "All three of them stormed into the room at once."

Manning looked suspiciously from side to side. "Three of them? Where's the third baby sleeping?"

McCarter jerked his thumb toward the ceiling. "Two floors above us in 1106. You can't miss him—he's the guy making puddles the hard way."

"You have been busy," commented the Canadian.

"I had help," McCarter said. "If Bobby hadn't been along, it could have been me upstairs."

"We helped each other out," the boy explained quickly. "I did what I had to do. What about the meeting? Are we going to get my dad back?"

"We may be getting closer," James said. "It's pretty much like we figured. The U.S. government has been given the opportunity to play in the same league as the Soviets. For transferring one hundred million dollars to a specified bank account in Mexico, we've been assured of your father's safe release."

Bobby Pearce frowned. "If America and Russia are both putting up the money, somebody's going to come up short. That means the United States could get left out in the cold. If it winds up that my dad does get taken to Moscow, then I'll have to dissociate myself from doing any more work on the SDI program. To continue on Star Wars under those circumstances would put my dad's life in danger."

"Sure," agreed Manning, "because eventually the Soviets would learn that the SDI program was still steaming ahead. That would tell Moscow they backed the wrong man, and then they would have little reason for keeping your father, well, for keeping him around."

"Exactly," the thirteen-year-old said. "Also, if I stop working on the SDI, it's going to put the implementation of the program right where the Soviets want it—at least twenty years down the road."

"I can't honestly tell you not to worry," Katz advised the boy, "but I do want you to know that we're going to do absolutely everything within our power to see to it that your father remains in the country and that he gets out of his predicament in one piece. If we have anything to say about it, though, by the time we're through, the Russians won't even be in the running for your father."

Hahn's face brightened. "Which would be especially true if we could stir up some friction between the Soviets and Robert Pearce's kidnappers."

"You have an idea?" McCarter asked.

Hahn nodded. "Perhaps. But first we must deal with an immediate problem." He pointed to the bodies slumped against the wall. "Obviously, our security has been violated and, unless I'm mistaken, we have a guest or someone employed here at the hotel to thank for that. We can no longer safely remain here without expecting more trouble."

"I was getting tired of this dump anyway," McCarter said. "What with the bodies, busted lamps and carpet stains, the mind boggles at such filth."

James clapped his hands together. “So let’s get packing.” He glanced to Hahn. “What about that idea of yours?”

“I’ll have to tell you later,” Hahn said. “After I’ve had a chance to do some shopping.”

"Ah, Senor Pearce, you are awake."

Robert Pearce blinked his eyes against the unaccustomed light as the stranger entered his cell. Pearce squinted and looked around him. He was no longer in the tiny room with the barred window. Sometime after his captors had pumped him full of whatever it was they were using to knock him out, he had been moved again. But where to?

His head felt like the inside of a cement mixer, but he could take the headaches. He could also handle the nausea and the foul, dry rot taste in his mouth. What he had trouble coping with was the uncertainty of what was going on.

He was used to being in control of his life. He functioned best when he was in charge. Now, the freedom that he had enjoyed most of his adult life had forcibly been taken from him and dealing with that fact was taking its toll on his nerves.

His new cell had no windows, only a small air-conditioning vent in the middle of the wall opposite his cot. Cool air pushed its way through the duct. The room's single light was recessed in the ceiling and protected by the grids of a metal screen. A woolen blanket was draped over his body, while his aching head rested upon a thin foam pillow.

The stranger opened the folding chair he was carrying and sat down beside Pearce.

"There," the man said, smiling. "Now we can talk. How are you feeling?"

Pearce licked his lips. "Thirsty."

"Of course you are," the man agreed without taking any steps to alleviate the problem. "I apologize for any inconvenience you have experienced during your stay with us."

"Spare me your sentiments, mister. I don't care what you're selling. I'm not in the market."

The man shrugged. "Very well. At least permit me to introduce myself, then. My name is Armando Torres-Quinteros."

"You already know my name," Pearce said sarcastically.

"Please, Senor Pearce, your poor attitude is not helping either of us. I came to inform you that your ordeal will soon be over."

"How soon?"

Armando Torres-Quinteros sat back and crossed his arms in front of his chest. "This is difficult to say, I'm afraid. If it were up to me, you would have left us long ago. Sadly, matters of such great importance take time. I can safely tell you, though, that you shouldn't be with us more than another day at the most."

"I'll believe it when I see it," Pearce scoffed.

Torres-Quinteros wagged a finger at Pearce. "That is precisely the kind of attitude problem I'm talking about. You are not helping the situation. Nevertheless, the reason I came to talk to you is that the terms for your release have been met."

"Then why am I still a prisoner?"

"Because I have a dilemma, Senor Pearce. You see, the terms have been met, but they have been met by the Soviet Union. You are, it seems, a most popular man."

Pearce digested this piece of news as though he were being forced to swallow spoiled meat. "So I'm bound for Moscow, is that it?"

"Not necessarily," Torres-Quinteros said. "I conferred with a representative of your government earlier today, and the United States has also agreed to our terms."

"What's your dilemma, then?"

"Strictly financial. Quite honestly, Senor Pearce, we would like to reach a compromise that will enable us to keep the payments made by both nations."

"It can't be done."

"Perhaps it can, perhaps not. In any event, the Soviets, as I said, have already met the conditions we've set for your release. While the United States has agreed in principle to those demands, they have yet to put their money where their mouth is. What do I do, then? Wait for your government to fulfill its promise to us, or do I go ahead and turn you over to the Soviets now?"

Pearce made himself smile. "Like you said, mister, it's *your* problem. Tell me, whatever happened to the short man with the thin mustache, the one who originally talked to me after I was abducted?"

"Why do you ask?"

"Just curious," Pearce answered. "The last I saw of him, he threatened to make me cooperate by kidnapping my son as well. Since I haven't seen him or my boy, I can only assume that your associate's threat was an empty one and that he failed to abduct my son."

"Don't be so sure of yourself, Senor Pearce." Torres-Quinteros scooted his chair back and stood. "Why do you think the Americans accepted our conditions for your release?"

The color drained from Robert Pearce's face. "If you really have Bobby, then show him to me."

Torres-Quinteros refolded his chair and turned to exit. "Maybe we will. Maybe we won't. Until then, I suggest you make yourself comfortable and get some rest. I'll send someone to bring you a glass of water."

The MERGE leader switched off the cell's overhead light and left Robert Pearce in darkness.

18

Phoenix Force waited at their new hotel room for Karl Hahn to complete his shopping expedition. Less than an hour after he left the group, the West German returned carrying two items. One resembled a portable sewing machine; the other was a small box. Hahn entered the room and crossed to a coffee table where he set down both items.

"Well," Hahn said, patting the larger object's high-impact, ABS plastic case. "Hopefully, with this, we will take a giant leap forward in shaking up the Russians."

"How?" McCarter asked. "By keeping the Reds in stitches?"

Manning shook his head and rolled his eyes. "It's not a sewing machine."

"Of course not," Bobby Pearce pointed out. "It's a portable computer."

"I knew that," McCarter insisted.

"Sure," Manning said.

"Does it have a name?" James wanted to know.

"A Bondwell 16," Hahn supplied. "A fine machine."

"With a nine-inch amber monitor, sixteen user programmable keys, a Winchester hard disk drive with a formatted capacity of ten megabytes, one single 5.25-inch floppy disk drive and a built-in, direct-connect modem with a three hundred-baud transmission rate," Bobby Pearce said, rattling off the personal computer's vital statistics like they were copied on the back of his hand. "And, for the icing on the cake, the Bondwell is also capable of synthesized speech."

"In other words, the computer can be made to talk," Katz concluded.

"Ja," Hahn said. "But what comes out of the Bondwell speechwise is only as intelligent as the thought put into its programming. Unless careful thinking goes into determining its choice of words, the resulting speech will sound silly."

Manning glanced at McCarter. "Are we still speaking about the Bondwell?"

"Pay attention," McCarter told the Canadian. "There may be a quiz later."

"Okay," James cut in. "We've got the PC. What're we going to do with it?"

"That remains to be seen," Hahn said, opening the small box he had carried in with the computer. Inside were ten double-sided, double-density floppy disks. "I have some ideas, and if Bobby doesn't mind giving me a hand, we just may be able to come up with something the Soviets won't like. Bobby?"

The Pearce boy brightened. "Anything, if it will help get my dad back."

Hahn smiled. "That's the spirit."

Late in the afternoon, Hahn and his able assistant triumphantly announced that they were ready to give Hahn's plan a try. The Bondwell was open and plugged in, with its internal modem—a device which enabled the PC to communicate with another computer—attached to the room's telephone line.

Hahn sat at the keyboard, his hands poised and ready to strike. "Thanks to Bobby's help I've been able to save many valuable hours from the time it would have taken me to translate my ideas into viable programs."

"Programs?" Manning repeated. "You've written more than one, then?"

"Altogether two," Hahn confirmed. "One to deal with the cheese; the other hopefully to lead us to the rats who want it."

Hahn inserted a 5.25-inch diskette into the Bondwell's floppy disk drive, then waited for the computer to boot up so it could go to work. Once the Bondwell was initialized, Hahn ran his fingers over the system's keyboard for a few seconds.

"Hello there," the Bondwell's computerized voice greeted them from the 16's front-mounted speaker. "What can I do for you?"

Hahn consulted the sheet of instructions Armando Torres-Quinteros had given James at their meeting, then fed a flurry of information into the portable PC. Immediately, a series of words and numbers flashed across the Bondwell's amber monitor.

"I'm having the PC search for the telephone line that connects with the Mexican bank's computer," Hahn explained.

"Beginning the search, thank you."

"Isn't it risky sending the call through the hotel's switchboard?" Katz asked.

"It would be," Hahn admitted, "if the hotel or the switchboard knew that we were doing it. We're bypassing such formalities."

"Once we find it," Bobby Pearce said, "we've programmed the Bondwell to try and gain access to the bank's computer system."

"Search completed, attempting contact."

More numbers danced over the Bondwell's monitor, and then the system emitted a bell-like tone.

"Contact established," Bondwell said. "What now?"

Hahn inputted his answer. "Since the Americans were given an account number to use at the bank, then the Soviets may been been given one, too. If that's true, then it's likely that both accounts were opened at the same time. We'll see. First, I'm having the Bondwell ask the computer in Mexico for the balance in our account."

Another chime sounded from the Bondwell's speaker, and then the portable computer said, "Account balance zero today. Do you want to make a deposit?"

"Okay," McCarter said. "So we've found out what we already knew—the account set aside for the United States is skint. What now?"

Hahn manipulated the Bondwell's keys. "Now we check the balances of the accounts immediately above and below ours. If the American and Russian accounts were opened simultaneously, the numbers for both should be consecutive. Right now, I'm examining the account which is numerically higher."

A figure appeared on the monitor, and Hahn punched one of the Bondwell's programmable function keys. "The numbers on the screen reflect the total amount of money on deposit in Mexican pesos. Bobby set the PC to automatically tell us how much that is based upon the bank's current exchange rate of pesos to dollars. Here it comes."

"Account balance fifty-six dollars and nine cents today."

"I think we're talking major slush fund here," James suggested.

Hahn blanked the screen. "Next we'll try the account which is numerically one number lower than ours."

He typed in the information, and within seconds, a long string of amber digits filled the 16's monitor.

"Looks promising," Katz said.

Hahn hit the programmable key again to get the peso equivalent in dollars. As soon as he did, the numbers on the screen disappeared and the Bondwell responded with its artificial voice.

"Account balance one hundred million dollars and zero cents today."

"All right!" James exclaimed. "That's it. The Soviet account. You guys did it!"

Bobby Pearce was all smiles. "We got lucky, that's all."

"Let's see if our luck holds," Hahn said, his fingertips inputting a new set of commands to the PC. "I'm directing the Bondwell to have the computer in Mexico transfer the money from the Russian account into ours."

McCarter laughed. "Can you do that?"

"We can try," Hahn said, keying in more instructions for the Bondwell to follow. "Now I'm checking the balance on the Soviet account again."

"Account balance zero today. Do you want to make a deposit?"

Hahn's fingers were a blur on the Bondwell's keyboard. "And now I'm checking the balance on the account set up for the American deposit."

In seconds, the portable computer provided the answer.

"Account balance one hundred million dollars and zero cents today."

Everyone cheered when the Bondwell finished speaking.

Katz looked from Karl Hahn to Bobby Pearce and then back to Hahn. "Brilliant. Absolutely brilliant."

"Hold on a minute, though," Manning said. "What's to stop someone from taking the money and transferring it back to where it came from?"

"It can't happen," Hahn said. "Bobby inserted a logic bomb into the program that prevents any unauthorized transfer of funds from taking place."

McCarter turned to Bobby. "What's this logic bomb?"

"It refers to secret instructions I've hidden in the program that will deny direct access to the U.S. account to anyone who doesn't know that the logic bomb exists."

"So since we're the only ones who know about it," Katz surmised, "the money stays put."

"Correct," Hahn said. "The bank's computer will show that the account contains one hundred million dollars, but that's as far as the computer will be able to interact with the amount on deposit. The money will be there, but even the bank won't be able to touch it. Essentially, the money is ours until we decide what we want to do with it."

"Nice work," James congratulated as Hahn's fingers began flying over the Bondwell's keyboard once more.

"That's one program down," Hahn said, "and one more to go." He nodded to McCarter. "Do you know anything about Tinkerbell in England?"

"I do if you don't mean the last time Peter Pan played the West End," McCarter said. "Tinkerbell is the ginormous computerized telephone-tapping system housed in the top two floors of the British Telecom building in London. Tinkerbell is voice-activated and programmed to recognize eighty percent of all words in the English language, in any accent.

"Tinkerbell means that thousands of taps can be set up without requiring somebody to actually listen on all of them all of the time. The system only starts taping a conversation after so-called 'danger words' are spoken.

"This worked fine until the big miner's strike a bit back. Some bloody fool decided to include 'picket' as one of the danger words; that triggered Tinkerbell's tape machines at least once every couple of seconds and wound up shutting down the system for a whole twenty-six minutes when Tinkerbell ran out of tape." The Briton grinned at Hahn. "That answer your question?"

"Indeed," Hahn said. "Impressively so."

"Not really," McCarter confessed. "I've got a subscription to *Private Eye*."

"Have you and Bobby rigged up a small-scale version of Tinkerbell, then?" Manning asked.

"Not exactly," the boy answered. "What we have done is tied into the telephone company's computer banks to automatically keep a record of any telephone number in the L.A. area that's used to place a call to the bank in Mexico City where our hundred million is deposited. If we know who's phoning the bank, then we may be able to determine where my dad is being held prisoner."

"In any event," Hahn continued, "it's the closest we've come to turning the tables on our opponents. Only time will tell if what we've done works."

"One thing's for certain," James said. "The Soviets are not going to be too happy when they discover their money's missing. I'd love to be a fly on the wall when that comes down."

"Yeah," Bobby Pearce beamed. "That's when it's really gonna hit the fan!"

19

Captain Oleg Lensky thought he was hearing things. Someone in the next room was singing the Soviet Army's favorite song "When the Tanks Go Marching In." Lensky realized as he jumped out of bed and threw on his clothes that the someone doing the singing was Major Kulik.

The KGB operative zipped his fly and stuffed the tails of his shirt into his pants and then hurried to see what was wrong with his superior officer. The singing grew louder as he made his way from his bedroom to the kitchen of the rented home.

The captain's mouth dropped open in surprise. There in front of the stove was Major Kulik. He was cooking eggs in one pan and frying bacon in another. Coffee was brewing in a percolator. Kulik cheerfully waved a wooden spatula in Lensky's direction and then proceeded to scramble the eggs to attention in time to the music.

"Are you feeling all right, Major?" Lensky asked, resisting the impulse to tap his feet to the beat of the familiar tune. "Is something the matter?"

"Bread's already in the toaster." Kulik stopped singing. "How about getting it going for me? I don't want the eggs to burn."

"Sure." Lensky frowned and then put the toaster through its paces.

Kulik flipped over the bacon. "I hope you're hungry this morning, Lensky."

"I imagine so, Major, but if you don't mind telling me, what is the explanation for your singing, your good spirits and preparing breakfast like this? As long as we've been here, you've never once fixed breakfast."

"Rotten of me, wasn't it, Lensky?" Kulik switched off the gas beneath the eggs and set the pan aside on an unlighted burner. "Of course, it was. The truth is, Captain, it's only this very morning that I decided it was safe to feel happy. We've met with the people who have Robert Pearce, we've satisfied their terms for releasing him to us and, by the day's end, Pearce should be in our custody and on his way to Moscow.

"What more could we ask for, Comrade? Our mission here in Los Angeles is on the verge of becoming a success. When we return home with Pearce as our prize, we shall be hailed as heroes." Kulik evenly divided the eggs onto a couple of paper plates, then did the same with the strips of bacon he had fried to a crisp. "Yes, Lensky, I said heroes. Something tells me that after what we have pulled off here, the Collegium will have no choice but to honor us as we deserve. Thanks to Robert Pearce, you and I are going places."

The toast popped up and Kulik quickly buttered both pieces. He placed the toast on the plates with the rest of the food, then motioned to Lensky.

"Shall we retire to the dining area, Captain?"

Carrying the breakfast, Major Kulik led the way, leaving the kitchen with Lensky following a few paces behind. A minute later, the two men were seated at a table enjoying their meal.

Lensky laughed as he devoured a mouthful of eggs. "You know, Major, being happy is not so terrible. Without a lot of difficulty, it is something I could get used to."

Kulik slapped his palm across the top of the table. "Ah, you see? I was right. And you feel it, too, Comrade!" He snapped his fingers. "I almost forgot, the coffee."

Lensky started to rise from his seat, but Kulik stopped him cold.

"No, no, Lensky. I will serve the coffee today. I'm feeling that good about the world."

Kulik set down his fork and pushed back his chair just as the telephone in the front room began ringing.

"Who can that be?" Lensky asked. "Not bad news, I trust."

"Never!" Kulik said, going to answer the call. "We are sailing the seas of victory, Captain. Nothing can stop us."

With that thought in mind, Kulik left Lensky sitting at the table and departed to the living room.

"Hello. Good morning," Kulik said into the phone.

"Good morning, Viktor. This is Armando. Remember me?"

"Remember you, my friend? How could I forget? And how are you faring this fine Tuesday morning?"

"Not as well as you, it seems, Viktor."

"I am sorry to hear that, Armando. A touch under the weather today, is that it?"

"You could say so, Viktor, but then having a business transaction that I believed in go unexpectedly sour like this would probably upset anyone. Hmm, Viktor?"

A train made of ice chugged into the depot of Kulik's stomach and parked. "Why, Armando, what on earth are you talking about? After we met your conditions so quickly yesterday, how can you possibly suggest that our business transaction has gone sour? We did meet your terms, didn't we? Or is this some clever trick on your part to make us pay more than the agreed-upon sum?"

"Your question is academic at this point, Viktor, especially after you and your friends saw fit to drain the bank account I set up for you of its last centavo."

"This has to be a joke, Armando. Are you mad? Out of your mind? Of course the amount we deposited is still in the account. We've paid dearly for a product, and we mean to have it."

"I see. Does that indicate, Viktor, that you intend to redeposit the specified amount a second time?"

"Absolutely not, you thieving bastard! I'm warning you—cross us on this and you won't live long enough to regret it."

"Such strong threats, Viktor. And after I thought we were going to truly be good friends. A pity. You really disappoint me. Adiós."

"Wait!" Kulik ordered and pleaded at the same time, but it was no use. The dead space at the other end of the line told him that Armando Torres-Quinteros had hung up.

It was then that Lensky chose to walk in from the dining room, munching on a piece of toast and wearing a broad smile.

"What was all the shouting about, Major?" Lensky asked. "Your breakfast is getting cold."

"Shut up, you moron!" Kulik snapped. "And get rid of that toast. We've got trouble."

Lensky's grin deflated faster than a politician makes excuses. "The phone call was bad news?"

"Worse. A disaster."

"Oh, no. Don't tell me that the Americans located Robert Pearce?"

"No," Kulik said. "I could live with that. The call I just received was from the Mexican, the miserable bandit I met with yesterday. He telephoned to say that the agreement to sell Robert Pearce to us is off."

"Off? But why?"

"Precisely what I put to that cheating dog of a liar. He claims his people are backing out of the deal because we changed our minds and removed the money that we had deposited for Pearce from the bank in Mexico City."

The half-eaten piece of toast fell from Lensky's hand to the floor. "He says the amount we deposited is gone?"

"Yes."

"Obviously, in spite of his assurance to the contrary, he is trying to double-cross us," Lensky concluded. "He's taken our payment for Pearce and then concocted this fable about us removing the money ourselves. He must be insane to think he can pull such a stunt and hope to get away with it." Doubt clouded Lensky's eyes. "Are you one hundred percent positive that the money is gone? What proof do you have?''

''Only Armando's word,'' Kulik admitted with a grumble. ''And right now, that crook's word is worth as much as having a freezer factory in Siberia. Armando may only be lying about the account being empty. That scum may be trying to trick us.''

Kulik unfolded a piece of paper that he had removed from his pocket, then lifted the receiver of the phone to place a call. ''There's one way to get to the bottom of this,'' he told Lensky, shaking the piece of paper in his hand, ''and that's to contact the bank in Mexico directly. We know where to phone, and we have the account number right here.''

The major stopped talking and made the call, waiting after it went through for someone who spoke English to be put on the line. When a female employee finally did offer to help him, Kulik quickly explained that he wanted to check the current balance of his account with the bank.

''May I please have the account number, sir?'' the woman requested.

Kulik told it to her, then whispered to Lensky, ''She's looking up our balance.''

The woman came back on the line. ''Hello, sir? Thank you for waiting.''

''No problem. Do you have my current balance?''

''Yes, sir, I do. Your account shows a zero balance today. Was there anything else?''

''No, I . . . thank you . . . I . . .'' Kulik's voice trailed off as he disconnected the call.

''Don't tell me, don't tell me,'' Lensky insisted. ''I don't want to know.''

"We don't have a kopeck in the account," Kulik said, completely ignoring Lensky. "One hundred million dollars on deposit and it is all gone." Kulik slumped onto the sofa. "We are ruined. That son of a bitch Armando has stolen our money and kept Robert Pearce, too. I'll kill him. I swear I will. He's dead, Lensky. Do you hear? I'll kill him. I'll strangle the life from his body."

The phone next to Kulik rang and he numbly brought the receiver to his ear. "Yes?"

"We're having a party and you're invited," a male voice informed him. "This afternoon at four."

The caller hung up and Kulik did the same.

"Good news travels fast, Lensky," the major told the captain.

"Oh, how I hate injustice," Lensky proclaimed. "What now, Major? What new horror do you have to reveal? Who was that on the phone?"

"Pack your bags, Lensky," Kulik said. "We are going home."

20

"Would you mind watching some television, Bobby?" Katz asked. The unit commander of Phoenix Force had just returned from speaking with Hal Brognola and was eager to share the details of that conversation with the rest of the team. "We won't be more than five minutes."

"No problem," the young computer genius said, going to the bedroom where the TV set was located. "Holler when you're finished."

Phoenix Force waited for the boy to close the bedroom door after him, and then Calvin James was the first to speak.

"So tell us. What did Uncle Hal have to say?"

"Plenty," Katz replied. "MERGE contacted Washington earlier this morning and confirmed the U.S. deposit of one hundred million dollars to the Mexican account. MERGE, it seems, is most anxious to conclude this deal and move on to bigger and better things."

"Terrific," Manning said. "If MERGE is getting cosy with Washington, it could indicate that the Soviets are no longer in the running for Robert Pearce."

"Plus," Hahn added, "that the trick we pulled yesterday of siphoning the funds from the Soviet account has worked to our advantage. Why else would MERGE push for a settlement."

"Karl's right," McCarter said. "MERGE has no reason to pretend they're on our side all of a sudden unless the United States is the only source of payment for Pearce now. Did Hal have any idea when we're supposed to receive the goods?"

"Midnight tonight," Katz answered for everyone's benefit. "In the parking lot of the Queen Mary. Calvin, you're supposed to be in the lot fifteen minutes early. Since MERGE thinks Gary is your driver, he's expected to be there, too. Neither of you are to be armed, and at the time Robert Pearce is handed over to you, MERGE is to be paid an additional ten million dollars."

"That clinches it, then," James said. "If MERGE is trying to squeeze more juice out of Washington, the Soviets are definitely out of the picture. This is MERGE's way of recovering some of what it's lost by losing the Russian money. Did Washington raise a stink when MERGE demanded the ten million bonus?"

"No," Katz said. "As far as MERGE is concerned, the U.S. is happy to make the additional payment so long as it means Robert Pearce will be safely released. Hal is arranging to have the ten million delivered to us here at the hotel."

"We may not need it," Hahn said.

"You had some luck with the Bondwell while I was out?" the Israeli asked.

"*Ja*, the program Bobby and I installed to retrieve local phone numbers that have been used to contact the bank in Mexico City has given us two possibilities to work with. Both calls were placed this morning within a half hour of each other."

"Have you had time to run down the addresses that belong to the phone numbers?" Katz asked.

"We were in the process of doing so when you returned," Hahn said.

"There's no point in having Bobby remain out of the room, then," Katz decided.

"I'll fetch him," McCarter said.

"How difficult will it be to determine the addresses, Karl?" Katz questioned.

"Not very." Hahn sat down at the Bondwell and began inputting instructions on the PC's keyboard. "We could find the general area that the numbers belong to by referring to the telephone directory, but even then we wouldn't have the exact information we need. Since we're already tied into the phone company's computer system, going through the Bondwell should provide us with what we want to know much faster. Right now, I'm requesting any available data relating to the two telephone numbers we have."

The West German stopped typing just as McCarter returned with Bobby Pearce.

"Any luck?" the boy asked.

"Checking one moment, please be patient," the Bondwell answered as though it had heard the question.

"We'll know in a moment," Hahn said.

"Still checking, thank you." The PC's bell-like tone sounded loud and clear from its speaker. "Requested information located and will begin receiving it at once." The Bondwell emitted a series of three loud beeps.

"Internal safeguard on contact computer prevents verbalization of requested information. Sorry."

"What's that all about?" McCarter wanted to know. "One second, our computer says its found what we're looking for; the next, it's refusing to tell us. How come?"

Hahn drummed his fingers in front of the keyboard. "There must be an antitheft program built into the phone company's data base. That would be the 'safeguard' the Bondwell mentioned."

A frustrating Manning complained. "Great. We've located the key to possibly getting to the bottom of all this mess, and now we can't use it."

"Perhaps we can," Bobby Pearce suggested as he crossed to Hahn. "May I?"

Hahn smiled and moved aside. "Be my guest."

The boy took a seat in front of the Bondwell, interlaced his fingers like he was about to begin a piano concerto and then attacked the portable computer in a flurry of keystrokes. In a matter of seconds, his performance was completed.

"Checking again, thank you."

"What I'm attempting is an override of the safeguard within the phone company's computer banks," the youth said. "The Bondwell told us the safeguard it encountered prevents it from verbalizing the information we're seeking, but that doesn't mean we can't ask Bondwell to come through for us another way."

The portable computer's familiar bell-like tone sounded again. "Requested information located and will begin receiving it at once."

"This is where we got hung up before," James said.

All eyes were glued to the Bondwell's monitor as a zigzagging amber line leaped across the screen. As soon as the flash of electronic lightning vanished, the first phone number Karl Hahn had tried to investigate appeared in the center of the screen. This information was immediately followed by the complete name and address of the party in the Los Angeles area associated with the number.

"The number belongs to a home in Pacific Heights," the boy read the information from the screen, "and it's registered to a Torres-Quinteros, first initial A."

"My old friend Armando," James announced. "Bull's-eye, Bobby!"

"Hold on." Bobby Pearce pointed. "Here comes the data on the second number."

But instead of being registered to a private residence, the owner of the phone was listed as a real estate agency in Culver City, a suburb of Los Angeles. In addition to the agency's address, a separate phone number was given.

"Why don't I give them a call?" James offered.

"Let me store this information before you do," the youthful computer wizard said, hitting the appropriate keys on the Bondwell's keyboard. As soon as he was finished, he signaled to James. "The phone's all yours."

Posing as a representative of the Federal Communications Commission, James called the real estate agency on the pretext of a violation of FCC regulations originating from a piece of property owned by the agency.

"Where's that?" the real estate agent asked from his end of the line.

James read off the phone number of the property in question, and the agent readily supplied the address that went with the number.

"Only it won't help you none knowing," the agent stated.

"Why's that?"

"The property was a rental. I had it out on a six-month lease to a couple of foreigners. I think they were Europeans. But you're a little late if they were up to pulling something fishy."

"You're saying they're gone?"

"You got it. Came in here not more than an hour ago, both of them crying and singing the blues about how they've got to hit the road earlier than expected and could they have their money back? I filed that one in the fat chance department. They signed for six months and paid for that privilege in advance. A deal's a deal. I told the pair no dice, and if they didn't like it, they could see me in court."

"And?" James prompted.

"And nothing. They weren't getting a dime out of me and they knew it. Right after I told them the facts of life, they split. I know they could have been on the level about needing the money, plus they were foreigners and all, but what the hell. A deal's a deal. Right?"

"Did the two men happen to say where they were going?"

"Afraid not, mister, I . . . listen, a customer just walked into the office. Can we cut this short?"

"My pleasure," James said. "And thanks."

James hung up and quickly relayed the gist of the conversation.

"It sounds like the Soviets operating the shop in L.A. have been recalled," Manning surmised. "I'd hate to be in their shoes."

"Yeah," McCarter agreed. "If I know Moscow, those shoes will be too tight to wear before long."

"Good," Katz said. "We can forget about the Russians and concentrate on this private home in Pacific Heights whose occupant is listed as A. Torres-Quinteros—in all likelihood the man we met with at the mall yesterday."

"I'm convinced of it," James said.

"It shouldn't be too terribly hard to find out," Hahn concluded. "I don't know about the rest of you, but I'm in the mood for a little drive in the car."

"Like somewhere in the neighborhood of Pacific Heights?" guessed Manning.

"Exactly what I had in mind," confirmed the former GSG-9 man.

"And what if it turns out that's where they're keeping my dad?" Bobby Pearce wondered.

"Simple," McCarter said. "We spring a visit on them later and clean house."

21

A preliminary recon of the Torres-Quinteros estate revealed almost exactly what Phoenix Force had expected to find. The drive past the sturdy iron gate leading into the property was made during late afternoon. McCarter was at the wheel of the Mercury, while Hahn rode along as the Englishman's sole passenger. The remaining members of the team had stayed at the hotel with Bobby Pearce.

"Not much to see," Hahn observed as they slowly drove by the gate. "I saw one man standing to the side of the main entrance, but that was all."

"I spotted him, too," McCarter said. "He hardly gave us a passing glance."

The gate was bordered on both sides by a red brick wall that was twelve feet high. Embedded in the top of the wall were curling barbed wire spirals. There were no trees within fifty feet of the brick barricade.

"For someone interested in this much security," Hahn said, "one would think Senor Torres-Quinteros would have more than a single individual guarding the front gate."

"You're right, Karl. The estate's apparent lack of protection doesn't make any sense."

McCarter braked and then executed a three-point turn in the middle of the road. He grinned at Hahn and started back toward the suspected MERGE stronghold.

"Where are we going now?" Hahn asked.

"I'm going to stop at the gate to the hacienda for a closer look. We'll put that one-guard theory of yours to the test."

Before Hahn could object, McCarter turned off the road and sent their car rolling up the short distance to the iron gate. No sooner had the Cockney commando slipped the transmission into Park than five armed Hispanics materialized on the opposite side of the gate.

"Sit tight," McCarter said. "I'm going to have a chat with them."

"Manning warned me there'd be days like this," Hahn admitted.

"Rubbish," the Briton said. "Gary was just pulling your leg. Back in a tick."

McCarter hopped from the Merc and walked boldly to the gate.

"What do you want?" demanded one of the gunmen. "This is private property."

"Not looking to buy it, mate," McCarter said, laying his East End accent on as thick as a double spread of Marmite. "Me and my pal in the motor here are looking for the Wiggins's residence. They're friends of ours from London. I was hoping you might tell us where they live? I had the address written down, but I guess I misplaced the bloody thing. Can you help me?"

"I have never heard of your friends," the gunman said, motioning with his weapon to the car behind McCarter. "Get into your vehicle and drive away now. Our employer does not like strangers."

"Nothing strange about me or my friend." McCarter smiled. "We're just plain, fun-loving folks."

"Then have your fun somewhere else."

The Englishman snapped his fingers. "Wait, I get it—the tough talk, the guns and all—you yobs are Hollywood actors! Right?" He stood on the tips of his toes trying to see over the shoulders of the man he was talking to. "Are they filming something for the cinema on the property?"

"Enough!" The MERGE hood lost his patience. "If you do not leave immediately, I will call the police."

McCarter presented his hands in mock surrender. "No coppers for me, thanks. I'm on my way. I don't suppose I could have your autograph, though? I've never been this close to—"

"Leave or I start shooting," the guard warned. "The police will believe me when I tell them you tried to attack us."

McCarter laughed at the threat. "And people ask me why I love California. Ta-ta, mate. See you on the telly." He spun on his heels and rejoined Hahn in the car. "Well, Karl, what do you think? Great performance?"

"Sure," Hahn agreed as McCarter backed the car out of the driveway, "Herr Laurence Olivier must be shaking in his boots."

"Let him shake," McCarter said.

Returning to the hotel, McCarter and Hahn lost no time in reporting what they had seen at the Torres-Quinteros estate.

"So Armando's little hideaway is under the protection of armed guards," James commented, speaking freely since Bobby Pearce was in the next room watching a game show.

"Five gunmen appeared at the gate right after Karl and I drove up," McCarter said.

Manning looked at Hahn. "And who's idea was it to stop at the gate?"

Hahn answered by momentarily shifting his gaze to the Phoenix team's U.K. representative.

"Say no more," Manning said.

"If Armando can spare five men for decorating his front gate," James continued, "then the rest of the grounds are likely to be heavily populated with unfriendly forces."

"True," Katz concurred as he turned to McCarter. "How much of the Torres-Quinteros residence is visible from the main entrance?"

"Part of the roof of the second floor and that's all," the Briton replied. "Not enough to matter. Too many trees in the way."

"MERGE has to be holding Bobby's father somewhere within the walls of the estate," Manning decided. "Why else would he have artillery?"

"Robert Pearce is in there, all right," Katz said. "And the trick will be to get in and get him out in one piece."

"Ideally," Hahn offered, "it would help if we could make an aerial study of the estate prior to taking any action, but doing so would be apt to arouse MERGE's suspicions."

"And prompt Armando and his bunch to move Robert Pearce to another location," James said. "Just what we don't want."

"So we'll hit the place and play it by ear," stated McCarter. "It won't be the first time."

"We know, we know," said Manning.

"The walls around the estate were about twelve feet high?" Katz asked.

"And topped off with barbed wire," Hahn told him.

The Israeli nodded. "Does that include the ocean side of the property?"

"As near as we could make out, the walls only surround three-quarters of the Mexican's estate," McCarter answered, lighting a Players cigarette. "The road leading up to Pacific Heights gave us a bit of a view as we were making our approach. Every home we could see on Armando's side of the street overlooked the beach. All of the homes are on cliffs. Some of the digs had stairs going down to the beach; a couple we saw had private lifts. Armando's place may have had both."

"Good," Katz noted. "The beach may be our avenue of entry."

"How close are the houses to each other?" asked Manning.

"Nothing for us to worry about," Hahn said. "Every home we saw was separated from its neighbor by a reasonable-sized stretch of land, either wooded or flowered."

"Umm-hmm." The brawny Canadian thought for a second. "The distance between Armando and his neighbors will give us a little more playing room and help confine the consequences of our activities to the property at large. That should keep the remaining Pacific Heights residents in the clear."

"If we were going for a clean sweep," Katz said, "we would hit the Torres-Quinteros estate with everything we've got and go for broke. A lightning strike in and out. Not knowing where on the grounds Robert Pearce is being held prisoner, though, eliminates such broad use of heavier hardware. Following that route could unnecessarily jeopardize Robert Pearce's life."

"How do you see us moving in, then?" asked Hahn.

"We could try and soft-shoe our way in," the Israeli tactician suggested, "but if the five armed guards at the front gate are any indication of the number of MERGE troops we are likely to encounter once inside the perimeter of the estate, then our chances of reaching our objective without bumping into the enemy are greatly reduced. My guess is that we're better off going in making noise."

"I like making noise," McCarter said.

"Good," Katz responded, "because you and Calvin are going to get to make a hell of a lot of it."

Low clouds hugged the coastline as Gary Manning, Karl Hahn and Yakov Katzenelenbogen cautiously made their way across the rocks and sand of the beach. Though the occasional star was visible overhead, for the most part the night sky was cooperating with their pending assault on the Torres-Quinteros estate.

To the right, the waves of the Pacific rolled and crashed, washing the shore again and again. The smell of salt was everywhere. On their left, jagged cliffs rose more than one hundred feet into the air. Staircases and the infrequent elevator car provided access to the homes above.

Having left Bobby Pearce under the protective custody of a couple of no-questions-asked agents at the Federal Building in Los Angeles, each of the Stony Man crew could devote his full concentration on the mission at hand.

The time was 9:37 P.M., which gave the three Phoenix warriors another eight minutes to get into place before McCarter and James went into action. In another ten minutes, Phoenix Force would bring hell to MERGE's doorstep.

Manning came to a rocky extension that jutted from the silhouette of the cliffs. Leaving Katz and Hahn behind, the Canadian warrior went to the edge of the craggy barrier; dropping to one knee, he peered around the outcrop.

Thirty yards farther up the beach, four MERGE gunmen congregated in a tight circle near the entrance to an open-air elevator car. The lax manner in which the four men gripped their weapons told Manning that although MERGE was prepared for trouble, it was obviously not expecting it. One of the guards was even enjoying a drink, tilting a bottle of unknown contents to his lips as Manning watched.

The Canadian pulled back and stood, then quickly retraced his steps to Katz and Hahn.

"We've got a reception party of four," Manning said, speaking in quiet tones that were instantly absorbed by the steady pound of the surf. "There's too many to get on my own without running the risk of at least one of them sounding some kind of alarm."

Katz tapped his noise-suppressed Uzi. "You take out two. We'll handle the others. How far away are they?"

Manning answered the question.

The Israeli nodded. "Let's do it."

Past experience with MERGE had shown the international criminal cartel to be a ruthless and vicious enemy. Prepared in advance for whatever MERGE might throw at them, all of the Phoenix squad members had armed themselves appropriately.

Besides his Anschutz air rifle with its NOD infrared scope, Gary Manning's battle gear consisted of a Desert Eagle .357 Magnum semiautomatic and a Smith and Wesson M-76 submachine gun.

Hahn's weapons included a 9 mm Walther P-5 worn in a shoulder holster and an H&K MP-5A3 machine pistol with a silencer attached to its barrel. Katz sported his Uzi plus a SIG-Sauer P-226 for backup. In addition to their regular combat equipment, each of the men carried a generous supply of hand grenades, both fragmentation and incendiary design.

Manning unslung the Anschutz and led the way back to the outcrop of rock where he lowered himself into a prone position and began lining up on the first of his targets. The Anschutz had an effective range of more than a hundred yards, which put the MERGE gunmen well within the air rifle's sphere of influence.

Utilizing steel darts powered by a CO_2 cartridge, the Anschutz could tranquilize or permanently dispose of an opponent with remarkable efficiency. Combining its payload with the air rifle's infrared scanner and Gary Manning's own skills as a sniper made the Anschutz one of the most important weapons the Canadian used.

Manning looked through the NOD scope at the guards and decided to pick off the one guzzling the bottle of booze. The scanner, which could amplify any available light up to sixty thousand times, revealed the label of the thirsty MERGE gunman's beverage to be that of a not so rare vintage called Mountain-Bird Wine.

Manning aimed, waited for his quarry to tilt his head back for a drink, then squeezed off a shot, embedding the steel dart from the Anschutz in the flesh of his target's throat.

The man froze in midswallow, and the bottle dropped to the sand. He staggered and clawed at the barb piercing his skin. As he sank to the beach like a deflating balloon, Manning sent an Auschutz night-cap into the next MERGE gunman in line.

As Manning began his attack, Katz and Hahn swept around the finger of rock to confront the remaining MERGE hoods. The three guards still on their feet were trying to unravel the mystery of their fallen colleague when the unexplained malady struck again.

Manning's newest target started to fall as soon as he was hit. One MERGE gunmen tried to keep the man upright. The remaining guard could not have cared less; he had more important things on his mind—things like stopping the pair of shadowy figures that raced at him out of the darkness.

The killer raised his SMG to fire. Katz beat him to the punch, spraying the gunman with a storm of destruction from his Uzi. Darks splotches appeared in all the wrong places as six 9 mm rounds connected with the Mexican's torso. The doomed man's chatterbox went flying and he began to dance, twitching and jerking to the Uzi's specialized tune, finally flopping to the surface of the beach long before Katz finished playing.

Using the body of one of his dead friends as an improvised shield, the final MERGE guard swung his rifle around trying to kill his enemies before they killed him. That desire died at the same time he did as Hahn unleashed the full fury of his Heckler and Koch machine pistol.

Bullets punctured the gunman's human shield and kept on going, plowing through the MERGE tough's chest and abdomen like deadly rockets coming up against a barrier of gauze. The killer's rifle fell from his grasp as a follow-up shot drilled a messy path between his eyes. Both he and his useless shield dropped to the ground locked in an embrace of death.

Katz and Hahn reached the base of the open-air elevator a few seconds before Gary Manning joined them. A quick check showed that all four MERGE guards were dead.

"Three minutes before the fireworks go off," Katz said. "Let's see what it's like upstairs."

Katz and Hahn entered the narrow elevator car. Manning slung the Anschutz over his shoulder and climbed aboard, too, pulling the lift's waist-high door shut and then pushing the up button. The elevator trembled and began to rise.

CALVIN JAMES AND David McCarter bided their time as they studied the iron-gated entrance to the Torres-Quinteros estate. The final minutes of their countdown were rapidly drawing to a close. Phoenix Force was about to throw a surprise party for MERGE.

Concealed in a wooded area across the street and directly opposite the same gate that McCarter and Hahn had stopped at earlier in the day, the British commando and his American counterpart were both equipped with choice party favors, not the least of which was a considerable assortment of hand grenades. When it came to surprises, the Stony Man duo had the market cornered.

Besides his Browning Hi-Power, McCarter also carried the Ingram MAC-10 submachine gun that had served him so well in the past. For a backup piece, he wore a .38 Special Charter Arms snubby tucked into a holster at the small of his back.

James's weapons were no less deadly. Beginning with a .357 Colt Python worn in a hip holster, his G-96 Boot 'n' Belt knife, and his Colt Commander, the former San Francisco SWAT team member was also armed with a Smith and Wesson M-76 SMG.

Unlocking any door requires some kind of key, and the one that James had brought along to deal with the problem of the iron gate was a beauty. The weapon was a Ring Airfoil Grenade launcher, developed by DARPA during the peak of the Vietnam War and then lost in a quagmire of red tape before it could be put to use.

The Ring Airfoil Grenade launcher's magazine contained five 53 mm rounds and, unlike an M-79 whose 40 mm grenades hit their objectives via a sharp trajectory, the aeroballistic construction of the RAG's doghnut-shaped projectiles permitted James to fire the launcher like a rifle. James and McCarter were hidden approximately one hundred fifty feet from the gate—no great shakes as far as the RAG was concerned since it had an effective range capability of thirteen hundred meters, better than fourteen hundred yards.

The plan for striking the MERGE stronghold was simple. While McCarter and James made noise at the front door, Katz, Hahn and Manning would slip in through the back. The hard part came once MERGE started making noise of its own.

McCarter looked at his watch and tapped James on the shoulder. "Fun and games time, mate," he whispered. "Ready when you are."

James grinned and whispered in reply, "I'm always ready."

The Phoenix team's U.S. representative set the RAG laucher's sights on the extreme left side of the gate where its hinges met the wall surrounding the estate. He took a deep breath, let the air out slowly and fired, sending a 53 mm airfoil grenade straight to its intended destination. James homed in on the far right side of the gate and fired again, getting the second RAG on its way a heartbeat before the first sailing projectile impacted against the gate and wall.

One deafening explosion followed another in a single continuous wave of thunder. The hinges on the gate proved no match for the RAG assault as brick and iron succumbed to the attack. The left side of the gate pulled away from the wall, then the right; its entire metal structure balancing on the ground for a second before crashing forward and across the drive.

The noise of the twin blasts had not completely faded when a gang of MERGE gunmen scattered like ants onto the driveway. Unlike the five men McCarter and Hahn had previously encountered, more than a dozen armed men poured through the wounded entrance to the property to investigate the disturbance.

The apparent honcho in charge of the group shouted something neither McCarter nor James could hear, motioning with his arm for the men to try to upright the remnants of the gate. Seven of those on MERGE's payroll hurried to obey the command, while the remaining hoods gathered in a tight cluster of guns and anxiety around the man calling the shots.

It was at that moment that James elected to let a third RAG air bomb take flight. Sighting on the energetic criminal spouting the orders, James fired, delivering the airfoil grenade to the center of the

MERGE tough's chest. The lucky guy never knew what hit him.

Bodies and parts of bodies flew everywhere. Some managed to scream before dying; most of those trapped within the radius of the explosion did not. A severed head bounced and rolled into the street. Bits and pieces of flesh splattered and stuck to the backs and faces of the men lifting the gate into place. An amputated arm became entangled in the coil of barbed wire on top of the wall, its weight causing the wire barricade to sag and the hand to wave up and down at nothing.

McCarter and James were running for the open entrance to the Torres-Quinteros property before the MERGE gunmen could recover from the effects of the RAG attack. James let the airfoil grenade launcher hang at his side, reserving the two 53 mm grenades remaining in its magazine for future use. The black Phoenix tiger wielded his M-76. McCarter gripped the Ingram M-10.

One MERGE gangster more alert than the rest screamed and pointed to the figures charging across the street. The problem from the gangster's point of view was that the pointing was done with his finger and not from the business end of his assault rifle. By the time he thought to correct that costly error in judgment, McCarter and James had opened fire.

The sharp-eyed gunman emptied his bladder as the first of many 9 mm slugs peppered his shrieking form. A furnace of pain lit his senses like a swarm of angry wasps nesting in his brain. He slipped to the pavement and sank to his death over the iron grillwork of the fallen gate.

One MERGE hood amazed himself by actually getting off a single shot with his revolver; but his surprise was nothing compared to that of the man next to him when the bullet from the six-shooter burrowed a hot tunnel through the hapless man's rib cage. The unintentional recipient of the .45 caliber missile died of a broken heart.

McCarter and James focused the attention of their weapons on opposing ends of the entrance to the estate, working their way to the middle ground between. Six MERGE guards were caught in the deadly crossfire of bullets that the Phoenix pair provided.

Three of the Hispanic hit men bought the *enchilada grande* when multiple wounds ruptured stomachs, perforated lungs and tickled testicles. Two more Torres-Quinteros tough guys bowed out with lead-lined skulls, while gunman number six spent the final seconds of his life skipping rope with his lower intestines.

McCarter and James ceased firing and took turns replacing the depleted magazines of their submachine guns. The leftovers of the Torres-Quinteros family littered the front of the drive. None of the killers guarding the gate would ever collect pensions.

"I hope Armando has plenty of dustbins," McCarter said, stepping over a body as he and James hurried through the gap where the gate had been. "The geezer's going to need them; there's nothing but garbage everywhere you look."

Shots rang out from the direction of Torres-Quinteros's home.

"Sounds like they started the party without us," James suggested.

"Not for long they ain't," McCarter said. "Let's go!"

Together the Phoenix Force superpros raced toward the gunfire.

23

The explosions had rocked through the interior of the MERGE stronghold like a low-level sonic boom.

"What the hell was that?" demanded the *jefe* of the Torres-Quinteros family, instinctively reaching for the Astra A-80 .38 Super semiautomatic he kept in the drawer of his desk. Armando Torres-Quinteros was discussing the scheduled 10:00 P.M. transfer of Robert Pearce to the American authorities with his nephew when the twin detonations went off. "It sounds like somebody's bombing us!"

Torres-Quinteros pushed away from his desk and quickly rushed to the double glass doors at the side of his office. He pulled them open and stepped onto a second-story balcony that faced the street. His nephew was close behind.

Someone had turned on the security lights. From their vantage point, they could clearly see beyond the trees in the front yard, but they could not see to the gate. Then another bomb blast erupted and a shock wave shook the balcony.

Torres-Quinteros angrily exclaimed, "We're under attack!"

"But who, Uncle?" his nephew cried. "The Americans?"

"No, it has to be the damned Russians! Somehow they've tracked us down and have decided to take Robert Pearce whether they've paid us for him or not. The fools! They'll never get past the gate!"

"Shall I order more men to assist our guards?"

"No. We have thirteen men posted at the gate... plenty to deal with the Soviet vermin."

The noise of the explosions died down to be replaced by the sound of a single gunshot. Then a chorus of screams reached the balcony and a feeling of dread washed over the MERGE boss like a shower of ice water in the dead of winter.

"I don't like it, Rinaldo," Torres-Quinteros said to his nephew. "One shot and next we hear men dying."

His nephew did not understand. "But why is that wrong, Uncle?"

"Because, Rinaldo, I think *our* men are the ones doing the dying!"

As if to confirm his assessment of the situation, a fresh round of weapon fire sounded from the ground floor of the very building they were in. The Russians had invaded his home. The Mexican Mafia chief reeled at this latest development, but that was nothing compared to how he felt when he caught sight of a pair of black-clad gunmen running up the drive from the gate, especially when he recognized the commando in the lead.

It was Senor Blue, the so-called representative of the United States government he was supposed to deliver Robert Pearce to later that night! Armando Torres-Quinteros trembled. That liar who called himself Blue and his companion were dressed like a couple of killing machines.

In a rage, Torres-Quinteros raised his Astra A-80 and fired three shots at the advancing duo, an impulsive gesture that nearly cost him his life. No sooner had Torres-Quinteros tried and failed to kill the commando pair with his Spanish semiautomatic than the balcony seemed to evaporate in a flurry of dozens of bullets.

Torres-Quinteros and his nephew turned and dove from the balcony to the floor of the Mexican's office. The doors behind them disintegrated in a shower of broken glass. One razor-sharp shard stabbed the wrist of the hand holding the Astra.

"*¡Vaya puneta!*" Torres-Quinteros swore, yanking the ragged sliver of glass from his flesh. Blood spurted from the wound at once. The MERGE chief sighed and decided it was not as bad as it looked and, pushing the pain he felt to the back of his mind, transferred the .38 Super to his left hand.

Gunshots were coming from the first floor of the estate on a regular basis now, a certain indication that Blue, or whatever his name really was, had brought along more than the one other commando Torres-Quinteros had seen. From the volume of hell he could hear happening below, it was obvious that the black American had numerous friends on the premises.

It did not take a genius to guess how fast and how far things had deteriorated. If Blue and one other could make it past thirteen armed men guarding the gate, then the Mexican wanted no part of the destruction that would surely find its way upstairs. *Better to flee and live to fight tomorrow than to stay and die today.*

Torres-Quinteros leaped to his feet and shouted to his nephew, "To the roof! It's our only chance."

"What about the Russians?"

"Not the Russians, Rinaldo. One of the men who fired at us just now on the balcony was the American we were supposed to deliver Robert Pearce to tonight."

"American?"

"Somehow they found us. Let's get to the roof before it's too late."

"What about Robert Pearce? Shall I—"

"There's no time. If we get him, they are sure to get us. Come!"

Rinaldo Orona-Torres pointed to the blood seeping from his uncle's wound. "And your hand?"

"A small matter," Torres-Quinteros answered, charging from the office. "I will live."

YAKOV KATZENELENBOGEN, Karl Hahn and Gary Manning came to the end of their elevator ride up from the beach just as Calvin James put the RAG launcher to work on the gate.

"That's our cue," Manning said as he jumped from the lift. "We're on!"

The three Phoenix Force fighters advanced undetected down the ramp leading from the elevator to the Torres-Quinteros household. The awning-covered passageway was bordered on both sides by night-blooming jasmine. No artificial lighting illuminated the narrow brick walkway.

As they progressed along the ramp, they heard another of James's airfoil grenades detonate somewhere in the vicinity of the gated entry to the estate. This was followed by a solitary gunshot and then nothing out of the ordinary. Since each of the submachine guns McCarter and James were using were noise suppressed, the lack of additional weapon fire was not a source of concern.

The brick sidewalk veered to the right and ended in a short stone stairway that led to the back door of the house. A bright, yellow light bulb burned over the screened entrance. The door did not appear to be locked.

Manning started down the steps and had just reached the bottom of the stairway when the screen door slammed open and two MERGE gunmen materialized on the back porch. Before they could react to the sight of the barrel-chested Canadian, Manning eradicated their expressions of astonishment with a couple of .357 Magnum erasers.

Twice the Desert Eagle cracked like portable thunder in Manning's fist. One MERGE loser overindulged to the tune of a single 158-grain semijacketed bullet, a severe weight imbalance that lasted as long as it took the back of the man's cranial cavity to erupt and paint the screen door with a gooey spray of blood, bone chips and brains.

The next Magnum-sized egg out of the Eagle was equally hard to digest, enlarging its target's mouth by six inches in all directions. The near-headless corpse collapsed at the knees and flopped on top of the body of the first killer Manning had disposed of.

"Passen Sie auf!" Hahn suddenly warned, raking his H&K machine pistol in a back and forth sweep that shattered a window on the second floor and enabled a lone MERGE rifleman to make an impromptu dive

that began with a scream and ended with a spine-snapping crunch on the bottom steps of the back porch.

"Thanks," Manning said, swiftly stepping over the bodies and pulling open the screen door to enter the home of Armando Torres-Quinteros. After he determined it was safe to do so, Katz and Hahn followed.

They were in a kitchen; a large four-burner gas stove dominated the room. A kettle was simmering on one of the burners, the contents of which filled the air with the aroma of tomatoes and onions.

A doorway beside the sink led around a corner and into a hallway. The three Phoenix Force warriors drew closer to the door. A babble of excited Spanish male voices was audible from beyond the far end of the corridor in another part of the house. Then the voices were lost in a fresh onslaught of gunfire.

"That'll be Calvin and David," Katz said. "Follow in five-second intervals so we're not clumped together."

Manning and Hahn nodded and watched as the Israeli disappeared through the doorway and started down the hallway. Hahn followed at the count of five. Manning was preparing to take his turn when the screen door behind him slammed open and three MERGE killers charged into the kitchen.

Instinctively, the Canadian dove through the doorway to the floor of the corridor, angry MERGE bullets chasing him as he dropped. Slugs chewed the door frame to splinters and sawdust. Manning hit the uncarpeted tile and slid out of immediate danger.

The Canadian daredevil climbed to his feet and sent two of the Eagle's best rocketing into the kitchen, the

Magnum deterrents designed to make the MERGE gunmen cautious of rushing into the passageway after him. At the end of the long hall, Katz's Uzi and Hahn's H&K came to life, exchanging shots of their own with MERGE.

Knowing it was impossible to continue without first dealing with the trio of thugs at his back, Manning removed a Mk3A2 offensive grenade from his arsenal, jerked the pull ring free and released its safety lever as he lobbed the grenade around the edge of the doorway and into the kitchen. Weighing 15.6 ounces, more than half of that being flaked TNT, the fiberboard, can-shaped Mk3A2's delay-detonating fuse took five seconds to explode.

The grenade transformed the kitchen into an instant chamber of death. Pots and pans fell from the walls in a chorus of metal striking the floor. The noise from the blast was reverberating about the room when at least one of the MERGE gunmen started screeching and squealing as loud as he could.

Gripping his .357, Manning returned to the kitchen. Two of the Torres-Quinteros family members were dead, both caught well within the Mk3A2's kill radius. The third MERGE mobster now had raw empty sockets instead of eyes. Blinded and bleeding, he was curled in a corner, thrashing in misery with the twin prongs of a ten-inch serving fork buried in his gut. The Canadian put an end to the killer's suffering with a mercy round to the head.

By the time Manning made it back to the hallway, both Hahn and Katz were gone, engaged in a firefight in some other part of the mansion-sized estate. To locate his friends, all Manning had to do was home in on the sound of the shooting.

This turned out to be the living room, which was a misnomer considering the pile of dead MERGE gunmen littering the carpet. As Manning entered the area, Katz and Hahn were trading shots with a couple of Hispanic diehards holding down the fort at the opposite end of the room. That was when McCarter and James appeared from a separate entrance, bringing the gun battle to a satisfying finish and reducing the final MERGE soldiers to a gruesome twosome.

"Is that the last of them?" Manning asked.

"Looks like it," McCarter said. "All except for Robert Pearce."

"And Armando," James added. "I haven't seen that weasel since David and I missed him on the balcony. He has to be hiding upstairs."

"I don't think so," Katz said.

Before anyone could ask for an explanation, the distinct noise of helicopter rotor blades whipping through the air filtered into the room from outside. The Stony Man supercrew raced to the manicured front lawn of the estate just as a two-man chopper lifted off the roof of the Torres-Quinteros home and took flight. Illuminated by the string of security lights stationed upon the roof, James had no difficulty identifying the whirlybird's passenger.

"It's Armando!" James shouted.

"And the pilot is the same guy Armando had guarding me at the mall," Manning pointed out.

James quickly unslung the RAG launcher from his shoulder as the chopper's rotors revved and the flying machine gained altitude. "I'm going to blow that sucker out of the sky!"

But instead of attempting to escape by heading out over the Pacific Ocean, the helicopter containing Torres-Quinteros and his nephew passed directly over their heads and flew to the neighboring property across the street where it hovered above the home. James imagined he caught a glimpse of Torres-Quinteros's gloating face, and then the chopper was up and away, lost in the darkness and the night.

"Damn!" James lowered the airfoil grenade launcher. "I couldn't shoot him and that bastard Armando knew it. I might have brought the eggbeater down on a bunch of innocent people. What luck."

"Never mind," Katz said. "We still have to find Robert Pearce."

They did that a few minutes later, locating the understandably grateful computer programmer within a tiny cell nestled deep in the basement of the former MERGE headquarters.

"I've got a million questions," Robert Pearce told the men of Phoenix Force.

Katz smiled. "And I know a boy named Bobby who can answer most of them."

Epilogue

Two days later, a frustrated Armando Torres-Quinteros left a bank in Mexico City and was killed while crossing the street.

A witness to the hit-and-run accident reported that he had seen a vehicle very much like the ones driven by foreign embassy officials flee the scene of the crime. The Mexican police elected to ignore the eyewitness account and looked elsewhere for clues.

HALF A WORLD AWAY IN MOSCOW, Major Viktor Kulik and Captain Oleg Lensky were presented with a gift from the KGB Collegium just as they were boarding the train for their new assignment in Siberia.

"What is it?" Lensky asked. "More injustice?"

"Let's see," Kulik said.

Carefully, the major unwrapped the lightweight package. Inside was a nicely folded copy of the *Los Angeles Times* dated the day before. Kulik opened the paper and took one look at its headline.

"I think," he told Lensky, "that we are going to be at our new assignment for a very long time."

"Why is that?"

Kulik refolded the paper and tucked it under his arm as he climbed aboard the train. "The headline tells the story of an incredible donation made to further the cause of freedom throughout the world."

"What are we to be blamed for now?" Lensky groaned.

"Yesterday an anonymous donor made a gift of one hundred million dollars in gold to support Radio Free Europe."

"I knew it," Lensky said. "More injustice, what did I tell you?"

"We do what we must," Kulik sighed. "This is our penalty for early withdrawal. Do you know that, Lensky?"

"Have you seen my mittens?" Lensky asked. "My hands are cold."